BOBBY
THE BRAVE
(Sometimes)

WRITTEN BY
LISA YEE

ILLUSTRATED BY
DAN SANTAT

Scholastic Inc.

New York Toronto London Auckland
Sydney Mexico City New Delhi Hong Kong

ISBN 978-0-545-05595-6

Arthur A. Levine Books hardcover edition designed by Elizabeth Parisi, published by Arthur A. Levine Books, an imprint of Scholastic Inc., September 2010.

12 11   16 17/0

Printed in the U.S.A.   40

First paperback printing, August 2012

TO SCOTT

Special thanks to Arthur Levine and Cheryl Klein, who love Bobby as much as I do.
Bon appétit to my mom and dad, who brought dinner over
when I was too busy writing to cook.
Kudos to Kait, who inspired the football-playing big sister,
and of course a huge shout-out to Benny,
who is my inspiration for Bobby.

TABLE OF CONTENTS

CHAPTER 1

He's Not Like You

DUCK!!!"

Bobby Ellis-Chan flung himself to the ground just in time. One second later and he could have been hit or even killed. Or at the very least, he might have lost an eye. There was no telling how fast that football was going.

"Son, are you okay?" a deep voice boomed.

As he rolled over and squinted up, Bobby could make out a giant silhouette looming over him. His dad was so big that he blocked the sun.

"Sorry about that," Annie said, rushing over and yanking her brother up off the ground. "But you walked right in front of us. That was dumb. Hey, are you okay? You look funny."

"I'm fine," Bobby insisted. His leg was sore and he had scraped his elbow, but he didn't dare let Annie know he was hurt or else she might call him a wimp. His big sister was brave and never complained when she was injured — like the time she broke her finger but refused to go to the doctor for two days.

Annie put her helmet back on and tightened the strap. "Dad and I were just throwing spirals. You want to join us?" When Bobby hesitated, she teased him, "Come on, it won't kill you. Football is fun!"

Bobby pretended to think it over before saying, "No thanks. Maybe some other time," which meant "never." He picked up his skateboard and hobbled toward his mom and Casey.

"Look!" Casey cried, holding up something wiggly and slimy. "A baby snake! Bobby, say hello to Snakey Snake Snake!"

"That's a worm," he pointed out. The worm looked distressed. "You'd better put it back."

Casey pouted. "But I want to invite Wormy Worm Worm to a tea party. Princess Becky says to be nice to nature." Bobby's little sister adored the TV show *Princess Becky's Planet* so much that she wore her Princess Becky costume and crown every day.

Mrs. Ellis-Chan set aside her basket of yellow and red zinnias. "Bobby, it looks like you're hurt," she said. "Let's get you cleaned up."

As his mother bandaged him up inside the house, Bobby could hear his father's booming voice outside.

"You've got a great arm, Annie!"

"That last pass was perfect!"

"You sure know how to make your father proud!"

Bobby winced.

"I'm sorry," his mother said. "Did I put the bandage on too tight?"

He shook his head. "It's nothing," he said. "I'm fine."

Bobby trudged up to his room and stayed there for the rest of the morning. He had important things to do, like drawing pictures of friendly aliens and their pets, cleaning his fish tank, and peeling off the sparkly stickers Casey had stuck all over his skateboard helmet. Finally, he decided to head to Holly's house and see what she was up to. Maybe he could talk her into going rock hunting. Or better yet, if he timed it right, maybe Holly would invite him to stay for lunch. Bobby was feeling a tad hungry, and Mrs. Harper, Holly's mother, made wonderful homemade bread and soup. She was the best cook. Everyone knew that.

Bobby's mom was back in the garden studying her flower bed. "It needs something," Mrs. Ellis-Chan mused. "But what? Maybe a small fountain or statue?"

Casey looked up with interest. "How about a castle?" she asked. "Or a moat. We should have a moat, then we could get an alligator and a whale, and Wormy Worm Worm could go swimming!"

"Be gentle with that worm," Bobby said. He didn't know much about worms, but he did know a lot about his little sister and how excited she could get.

"I *am* gentle, Bobby," Casey insisted. "Look! Wormy Worm Worm is hugging me!" Sure enough, the worm had curled around Casey's finger.

Bobby stepped onto his skateboard and pushed off. He breezed down the driveway and did an impressive ollie along the way, getting high in the air. The thought of a big bowl of Mrs. Harper's soup was making his stomach growl.

Mr. Ellis-Chan and Annie were laughing and talking

as they did push-ups on the lawn. "That Bobby," he over-
heard his father say when he skateboarded past, "he's not
like me."

"That's for sure," Annie answered.

Suddenly, Bobby wasn't hungry anymore.

CHAPTER 2
The Class Musical

On Monday morning, Holly was waiting on her front porch. She leapt up when she saw Bobby. They high-fived with their right hands, high-fived with their left hands, stuck their thumbs in their ears, wiggled their fingers, and shouted, "Whoop! Whoop! Whoop!"

When they finished their supersecret greeting, Bobby noticed that Holly had combed her hair again. It was a useless habit she had picked up over the summer, and that was over a month ago. If that weren't bad enough, today Holly was wearing a pink dress. Bobby tried not to shudder. Not only did dresses make Holly look like a girl, but pink was his least favorite color. Bobby's most favorite color was cerulean, a darkish shade of blue. He loved saying *cerulean*.

Cee-roou-lee-an. *Cerulean*. Cerulean.

Bobby even had a cerulean paint chip from when he went to the hardware store with his dad once — just the two of them. Afterward, they feasted on glazed buttermilk donuts at Benny's Donut Palace. That had been a great day.

"Is that what you're wearing for the class picture?" Holly asked.

"That's today?" Bobby had forgotten all about the class picture — not that he would have dressed any differently. "What's wrong with my clothes?" Bobby sniffed his Troy Eagle skateboard T-shirt. He had about one hundred Troy Eagle shirts. Well, if not a hundred, then at least seven, one for each day of the week. His shirt didn't smell too bad. Bobby's father was in charge of the laundry, which meant that it didn't always get done.

Mrs. Ellis-Chan worked at an office, while Mr. Ellis-Chan stayed home and took care of Casey and the cooking and cleaning. Three years ago, when he was the star linebacker for the Los Angeles Earthquakes, a National Football League team, Mr. Ellis-Chan could count on a football arena filled with cheering fans. These days, the only thing he could count on were laundry baskets filled with clothes to be washed. Still, he claimed to love being a stay-at-home dad, even if it was "a lot harder than playing pro ball."

"Never mind," Holly said as they walked toward school. "If you stand in the back when they take the photo, the wrinkles won't even show. So, what about the class musical? I can't wait to find out about it!" When Bobby didn't respond, she asked, "Aren't you the least bit excited?"

"Nope." Bobby shook his head. He stopped to pick up a small black rock and slipped it into his pocket.

"Well, why not?" Holly asked. "It's going to be so fun."

Singing, dancing, and embarrassing yourself in public were not Bobby's idea of fun. Fun would be painting the garage with his dad, or skateboarding, or rock collecting.

Holly was still talking about the class musical when they neared the Parting Place. At Rancho Rosetta Elementary School, it was considered weird for fourth-grade boys and girls to be friends. Not too long ago this is where Bobby and Holly would have split up so no one would see them together. But they marched right past the Parting Place. Ever since Bobby and Holly ran against each other for student council representative, they were determined not to let what other people thought bother them. Well, not too much.

As they approached Mr. Kirby, the ancient crossing guard, he slowly rose from his lawn chair and gave them the peace sign. Gently, Bobby and Holly helped him across the street, then they ran to the playground, where Bobby joined the boys and Holly joined the girls.

Mrs. Carlson was writing the date in cursive on the whiteboard. Bobby admired his teacher's handwriting. It was pretty and precise, like her. Mrs. Carlson looked especially nice for picture day and had a real flower pinned to her sweater. Bobby tugged on the collar of his shirt and noticed that it was crusty where some food had dried.

Lots of the girls were wearing party clothes and had done complicated things to their hair. Bobby noticed that some of the boys didn't look normal either. Jackson's hair was plastered down and combed to the side, making him look like a dork. Chess, Bobby's other best friend besides Holly, was wearing a long-sleeved shirt and a tie. Bobby didn't even own a tie, or a long-sleeved shirt, although he did own a pair of gold antique cuff links that Gramps had given him.

The morning flew by. In social studies, Mrs. Carlson talked about freedom of speech. "We are lucky to be American citizens because we have the right to express ourselves. In some places, people can get sent to prison just for saying something that the government doesn't agree with. It's called *oppression* when people are unjustly punished for speaking out, and those who do it are oppressors."

Without warning, St. James stood on his chair and yelled, "I am the king of everyone!"

"Please step down, St. James," Mrs. Carlson said. She acted like she couldn't hear the entire class roaring with laughter. When he continued standing on his chair, Mrs. Carlson crossed her arms. "NOW," she ordered, "or you will be sent to Principal Coun's office!"

"I was just expressing myself," St. James muttered as he sat down.

Jillian Zarr and the rest of the girls glared at him. They would make good oppressors, Bobby noted.

"Now for something really fun," Mrs. Carlson announced. "As you know, every year my class puts on a musical. This year's show is *Annie*!"

Bobby raised his hand. "Annie is my big sister's name," he said proudly.

"It's a lovely name," Mrs. Carlson told him. When she smiled, Bobby felt good — important, even.

Mrs. Carlson went on to tell her students that *Annie* was about a spunky girl who lives with the evil Miss Hannigan in an orphanage. During the show, Annie befriends a dog named Sandy, and is later adopted by a rich man named Daddy Warbucks.

"In the Broadway musical, all the orphans are girls. However, in our Rancho Rosetta version, the show will be much shorter, plus our orphans will be boys and girls. Here is the sign-up sheet and a list of parts you can play. Write down your first, second, and third choices," Mrs. Carlson instructed. "And remember, this show isn't about who's the best singer or dancer, it's about all of us having fun and working together."

The room suddenly got loud as the sign-up sheet made its way around the class. Several girls wanted to be Little Orphan Annie, and lots of the boys wanted to be Daddy Warbucks. Bobby just sat on his hands and studied the crack in the ceiling. It looked like a spider with five legs. He didn't want to be in the musical at all, unless, of course, he got the only role worth playing. But with his luck, that was sure to go to someone else. Last year, for his third-grade play, Bobby was a tree, and not even one of the trees near the front of the stage. He was a back tree.

"All right then!" Mrs. Carlson said. "I'm going to review the list. If more than one person has signed up for a particular role, I will draw names. After recess I'll post the results. Remember, we'll be taking our class photo later this afternoon. So try not to get your clothes dirty."

The boys raced to the handball courts, while the girls gathered in clumps on the playground. Bobby lost his first three games, but won the fourth one against Chess when he hit a spectacular low ball. Handball wasn't nearly as dangerous as softball, basketball, or especially football. As far as he knew, no kid had ever been seriously injured playing handball. In football, players were always getting hurt.

Bobby could remember going to his dad's LA Earthquakes games when he was little. Whenever his father was tackled, Bobby would hold his breath until he got up and waved to show he was okay.

Later, as the class piled back into the room, everyone pushed forward to the bulletin board where Mrs. Carlson had posted the *Annie* assignments.

"All right!" St. James yelled, pumping his fist in the air. He was Daddy Warbucks.

Chess and Jackson were orphans, and so was Jillian Zarr. Holly was Miss Hannigan, and Swoozie, a girl who barely spoke, had the title role of Annie. Bobby scanned the list for his name, and when he saw it, he lit up. He got his first choice: Bobby would play Sandy, the dog!

CHAPTER 3
Say "Cheese!"

Throughout lunch, Bobby barked and romped and panted. It was, he knew, important to rehearse being a dog so he could get it just right. Several times his friends joined him. It was fun making the first graders scream and seeing how fast they could run.

Later, during afternoon recess, the boys played one of Bobby's favorite games: Arctic ice robots. They were frozen and trying not to melt when Jillian Zarr and her wolf pack circled them.

"Hey Bobby, your shirt is all wrinkled and it's on backward," Jillian Zarr said. She picked a piece of lint from her ridiculous dress, which looked like a giant pineapple.

Bobby shrugged. "So what?"

"It's inside out too," Jillian Zarr pointed out. "Do you still need someone to dress you in the morning?"

All the girls started giggling, except for Holly. She had
never been a giggler.

"I wore it this way on purpose," Bobby lied, fixing a steely-
eyed glare on Jillian Zarr, the way he had seen his father do
when he wanted to freak out the opposing football team. The
truth was, Bobby never bothered to check if his clothes were
inside out, or outside in, or whatever they were supposed to
be. There were more important things to do in the morning,
like feed Koloff and Beatrice, his fish.

"Why would you want to wear your clothes all weird?"
Jillian Zarr asked. Her eyes narrowed.

Bobby blinked and looked away. He opened his mouth, but nothing came out. Luckily, Chess spoke up. "Maybe Bobby's starting a trend."

"A trend?" Jillian Zarr threw her head back when she laughed. She was the only person Bobby knew who did this, other than the evil genius from that movie *Kid Kops*. "That's not a trend, that's a dumb thing to do," she said. "Besides, Bobby Ellis-Chan is so NOT a trendsetter. If you looked up 'not a trendsetter' on the computer, Bobby's name would come up."

Bobby could feel his face turning red. He hated Jillian Zarr with all of his heart, and even more. He hated her with all of his heart, and his arms and legs, and even his ears and nose.

"Bobby's a total trendsetter," St. James shouted. By now, all the boys had ceased being frozen Arctic robots and transformed into angry fourth graders. "Hey guys, follow me!"

Before Jillian Zarr could reply, there was a great stampede. All at once the boys ran away, leaving Bobby alone with the girls. Had his friends abandoned him? he wondered. What was so bad about a backward, inside-out shirt?

Bobby squirmed as the wolf pack circled him in silence. He knew from his report about wolves last year that the circling meant they were going to attack soon. Then, as quickly as they had disappeared, the boys came running back. Bobby felt a wave of relief wash over him — he hadn't been abandoned! The girls didn't dare rip him to pieces when he had backup.

Bobby's heart swelled. St. James, Jackson, and the others had turned their shirts backward and inside out to match his! Right then and there, Bobby decided he would do anything for them.

Anything.

"I suppose you all think that's funny," Jillian Zarr said.

Bobby grinned and glanced at Holly, who was trying to hide her smile.

"It *is* funny," St. James said, making a pig nose. "And so are you! Oink! Oink! Oink!" Soon all the boys were oinking, and the air was thick with pig sounds, and an occasional moo and bark, as Jillian Zarr and her wolf pack retreated.

"Hey, guys," St. James announced when the animal noises finally stopped. "Besides the backward, inside-out shirts, I know how we can make our class photo even better."

As they listened to his idea, everyone grinned. "That's going to be awesome!" Jackson crowed.

"Yeah," Chess chimed in. "It's the best!"

"Are you in?" St. James asked Bobby.

Bobby gulped and then put on his best fake smile. "Oh, sure," he said, remembering he'd do anything for his friends. Anything. "I'm in all the way!"

A red felt hat boasting a spray of colorful feathers perched on the top of the lady's head. The photographer waved her arms to get everyone's attention, and Bobby thought she might fly away.

"Okay, you good-looking kids, come over here!" she called. "Let's see if you can follow orders better than the third graders!"

Everyone laughed. Third grade was so last year.

In an orderly manner, the fourth graders of Room 15 walked to the risers in a straight, single-file line. Once everyone was in place, St. James tapped Bobby on the shoulder and whispered, "Remember what we're supposed to do." Bobby nodded. He didn't want any of the guys to think he was a party pooper.

"Okay!" the photographer yelled. She honked a bicycle horn to get everyone's attention. "Look at the feathers on my hat, and on the count of three say 'CHEESE.' One . . . two . . . wait a minute!"

Everyone held their frozen smiles as the photographer squinted. "You there, and you and you and you," she said, pointing at several boys. "Your shirts are on backward and inside out. I can see the tags in the front!"

Bobby and the others shifted nervously.

Mrs. Carlson surveyed her class. "Boys," she said, shaking her head. "You have exactly two minutes to step outside and fix your shirts."

Even though Jillian Zarr was in the back row, Bobby knew she had a smug smile on her face.

The boys began to stomp down the risers and make their way out of the auditorium, when Chess suddenly stopped and declared, "Freedom of speech!"

Everyone looked surprised.

"Freedom of speech," he repeated. "Mrs. Carlson, you're teaching us about freedom of speech and expression, and this is one way we're making a statement."

Mrs. Carlson asked, "Chess, exactly what statement are you boys trying to make?"

"I don't know," Chess said, pointing to Bobby. "Ask him. He started it."

The rest of the boys nodded and pointed to Bobby.

Bobby wanted to pull his shirt up over his head and hide. Finally, he stammered, "Um, the freedom to, um, to wear clothes however?"

Could he go to prison for this? Bobby wondered. He imagined himself behind bars with nothing to eat but stale bread crusts and brown water.

Chess jumped in. "See, it's our right as American citizens to express ourselves by what we wear."

Mrs. Carlson laughed. "Well, you do have a point. And your clothes aren't offensive. I'll tell you what. . . . If you think your parents will be okay with it, then I will be too. Now then, back into position, everyone!"

"Are you sure?" the photographer asked.

Mrs. Carlson nodded. As Bobby exhaled, the boys grinned at each other and the girls frowned.

"Don't forget, we're still doing what we promised to do," St. James whispered.

Bobby was game for anything now. So when the photographer counted "One . . . two . . . three!" he made the silliest, goofiest face he could.

CHAPTER 4
Mr. Wiener House

As they gathered around for dinner, the Ellis-Chan family all talked at once. Sometimes it was hard to get a word in, but Bobby was used to that.

"I want to get some clean dirt for Wormy Worm Worm," Casey was telling her mother. "The dirt he has now is all dirty."

"Then what did your coach say?" Mr. Ellis-Chan asked Annie. He could get very focused when talking football.

"Coach says that I have a great throwing arm, but that I need to practice more." Annie stopped talking just long enough to poke her father's double crusted mac 'n' cheese 'n' cabbage 'n' carrots.

"I'm going to be Annie's dog," Bobby volunteered. When no one paid attention, he repeated himself louder. "I'm going to be Annie's dog!"

His big sister frowned. "I don't want you to be my dog."

"No, I'm going to be in the musical about Little Orphan Annie and play Sandy, the dog."

"Oh, that's wonderful," his mother said. "Bobby, you'll make a great dog. I just know it."

Bobby felt warm inside. It was true, he thought. He'd make the greatest dog, not just in the entire world, but in the entire solar system. Bobby loved dogs and even considered himself an expert on all things dog. If he didn't have asthma and wasn't allergic to fur, he would have five dogs, maybe ten or even twenty.

"Dad, did you hear? I'm going to be a dog!" Bobby took a bite of his father's latest creation and then quickly drank some milk.

"What if we had a more regimented series of backyard drills?" Mr. Ellis-Chan asked Annie. "I can even show you some we used to do when I played for the Earthquakes."

"Cool!" Annie said. "Can we do it right after we finish eating?"

"Of course," her father replied. "I love it that you're living your dream. Wow, my daughter is quarterback of the high school football team! Have I told you how proud I am?"

"Yeah." Annie laughed. "Like about a million times!"

"Dad?" Bobby said meekly. "I'm going to be a dog."

But his father was too busy talking to Annie to hear him. Why would he even care that his son was going to be a dog when his daughter was a football star?

Later, as Mr. Ellis-Chan guided Annie through her football drills, Bobby watched them from his bedroom window. "He's not like me," Bobby recalled his father telling Annie. What exactly did that mean? That Bobby wasn't as brave as his father? That he wasn't as athletic as his father? That he wasn't as popular as his father? That he wasn't as big and strong as his father?

Bobby's shoulders slumped. It probably meant all those things and more. The two of them couldn't be more different.

Over in the garden, Bobby could also see his mom tending to her zinnias and Casey talking to Wormy Worm Worm.

"Look, I brought you a present," his little sister was saying. She loved giving presents and just yesterday had insisted that Bobby keep the butterfly barrette she gave him. He smiled as

Casey tried to coax her worm into sitting up straight in a doll-house chair.

"Great job!" Mr. Ellis-Chan yelled to Annie when she mowed down all the empty cans on the brick wall with her throws. "Oh man, you were right on target every time. Let's see that again; I know you can do it!"

Bobby closed the window and then retrieved his wooden cigar box from his bookshelf. It housed some of his most valuable possessions: Gramps's gold cuff links; an odd-shaped piece of metal, possibly from an alien spacecraft; a photo of Mr. Ellis-Chan holding the two-year-old Bobby in a football jersey with the entire LA Earthquakes team surrounding them. Bobby found what he was looking for under a broken stopwatch.

Gingerly, he took out the tiny soccer ball and cradled it in the palm of his hand. It was about the size of a marble and had belonged to Rover. Rover had been Bobby's beloved goldfish, but he had died in a tragic bubble-bath accident. It still pained Bobby to think about it.

As Bobby dropped the soccer ball in the aquarium, Koloff and Beatrice swam away from it. "Come on, you two, try to push the ball!" Bobby coached. "Rover loved playing with his soccer ball. He could push it all around the tank and even get it into the soccer net. Give it a try. Come on, I know you can do it!"

Koloff and Beatrice did not seem interested. Not even Diver Dave, the plastic diver who swam up and down, up and down, wanted anything to do with the ball.

"Okay then, how about this?" Bobby said, giving them hand signals. Rover had been able to follow Bobby's commands to swim though hoops and in circles. When Koloff and Beatrice didn't respond, Bobby gave up.

"That's okay," he assured the fish. "Sometimes these things take time."

"Mmmmmmmmm . . ."

The morning started off great. At the urging of his family, Mr. Ellis-Chan served his delicious homemade cinnamon rolls for breakfast. It was the one thing he made that the entire family loved. "Mmmmmmm," Bobby said again as he took another bite. "Dad, you should make your cinnamon rolls for every meal!"

"Thanks, son," his father said, beaming.

At school, Mrs. Carlson taught the class the songs from *Annie*. Bobby was glad he didn't have a solo; pretending to sing along was hard enough. Jillian Zarr's singing sounded just like her talking, except louder. St. James was a terrible singer, but he didn't seem to notice. Holly was great as Miss Hannigan and had everyone laughing, especially because Miss Hannigan was mean and Holly was always nice. But the big surprise was Swoozie. Bobby had hardly noticed her before. She was just one of the girls in Jillian Zarr's wolf pack. Yet when Swoozie sang, it was like she was someone else entirely. She was a star.

Bobby wondered what that would be like — to be a star. His dad was a famous ex-football player, and Annie was the star of her high school football team. His mom was a star at her company, Go Girly Girl, and had been named employee of the month twice. Even Casey had people fawning over her wherever she went because she was so cute. But Bobby, well, he was just plain Bobby.

Later, during lunch, St. James asked, "If you could have one superpower, what would it be? I'd like to fly." To prove this, he jumped up and, with his arms extended, ran around the lunch tables until a lunch lady made him stop.

"I'd read minds," Chess said as St. James was getting lectured.

"I would be invisible," Jackson said, nodding. "Yep. Invisible, so I could spy on people. Either that or be a diabolical super genius. What about you, Bobby?"

"Superhuman strength," Bobby answered. He imagined himself making the winning Super Bowl touchdown as his father cheered, "That's my boy — I am so proud of him!"

"Superhuman strength?" St. James repeated when he was allowed to sit back down. "That'll come in handy in PE. Did you hear? We got a new PE teacher. And get a load of this, his name is . . . Mr. Wiener House!"

"Wiener House?" Jackson said, laughing so hard that milk almost came out his nose.

"Yeah, Wiener House!" St. James said as the boys cracked up.

"Wiener House! Wiener House! Wiener House!" they chanted as the bell rang.

As the students of Room 15 stood in straight rows on the playground, their new PE teacher looked them over and frowned. Bobby thought Mr. Wiener House looked mean, like that man in the bathtub cleaner commercial who scrubbed away stubborn dirt and soap scum.

"When I call your name, say 'here,'" the PE teacher ordered.

"Amy Aoki?"

"Here."

"Jackson Chavez?"

"Here."

"Robert Ellis-Chan?"

Bobby gulped. "Um, excuse me, Mr. Wiener House? Can you call me Bobby instead of Robert?"

Bobby watched as the new PE teacher's face went from pale to pink to a deep dark red. "What did you say?"

Bobby felt himself shrink. "Bobby. If you could call me —"

"What did you just call me?" the teacher boomed.

"Mr. Wiener House?"

All the kids were snickering, especially St. James.

"It's Rainerhaus. My name is Mr. *Rainerhaus*. It's pronounced Rain-er-house. And you, Robert, can sit on that bench for the rest of PE. I will not tolerate smart alecks!"

Bobby glared at St. James as he made his way to the bench. St. James was famous for stirring up trouble, and usually Bobby thought it was funny — except when he was at the center of it.

Sitting alone, Bobby watched his class play soccer. They looked like they were having fun. His dad would never have let himself get tricked like that. Bobby was glad his father wasn't there to see him sitting on the sidelines.

CHAPTER 5
Scary Cat Attack

That afternoon when Bobby got home, Casey was outside explaining leprechauns and rainbows to Wormy Worm Worm. Bobby waved hello to her and went on into the kitchen, where he found his father.

"Hi, Bobby!" Mr. Ellis-Chan said as he rinsed the mixing bowl. "How would you like to be the first to try my blueberry-tomato cookies?"

Bobby looked at the lumps on the plate and shook his head. "No thanks, Dad. Maybe later."

For a split second his father looked disappointed. But he quickly composed himself and asked, "Everything okay, son?"

"Everything's just fine," Bobby said as he rushed to his room. He couldn't bear to tell his father about what had happened in PE.

Koloff and Beatrice were swimming back and forth. Diver

Dave was swimming up and down. Bobby watched them for a while before releasing a huge sigh. "I got in trouble at school today and had to sit on a bench during PE," he confessed to them. "You probably have no idea what it's like to be stuck in one spot for a whole hour."

Beatrice stopped swimming and then began to circle the tank. She was a pretty white fish with orange spots. Koloff, who was all orange, was skimming the rocks on the bottom of the aquarium.

Bobby leapt up. "Oh my gosh, you *do* know. You're stuck in this aquarium all day and night." He paced his room. "Wait," he said as he ran his hands through his hair. "Just because I was benched doesn't mean you have to be too!"

"What are you doing with that spoon?"

Casey looked up at Bobby. She had dirt on her face and all over her gown. "Digging a lake for Wormy Worm Worm. Want to help?"

"No thanks," Bobby said. "Hey, can I borrow your Princess Becky wagon?"

"What for?" she asked as she emptied a cup of water into the hole.

"I want to take the goldfish for a walk," Bobby explained. "They don't get out much."

"Fishy Fish Fish and Fish Fishy Fish?" Casey said.

"They have names, you know," Bobby grumbled. It bugged him that she was always making up dumb names. "It's Koloff and Beatrice." Those were great names. Koloff was named after the amazingly sticky and stinky Koloff tree at the Huntington Gardens. Bobby knew that tree really well, having been stuck to it on a class field trip. Beatrice was the name Holly had given the other fish. Technically, Beatrice belonged to Holly, but really she was both of theirs.

"Okeydokey, Koloff and Beatrice. Don't be mad, Bobby."

Instantly, Bobby felt guilty that he had snapped at Casey.

"Bobby, can Wormy Worm Worm go for a walk too? He doesn't get out much."

Bobby nodded. If that was the price of borrowing her wagon, then it would be worth it. He had considered balancing the fishbowl on his skateboard and pulling it with a rope, but that seemed too risky. Yes, the wagon was the best form of transportation. After all, didn't the settlers cross the plains in covered wagons? Bobby imagined his fish were the pioneers and he was the horse.

There was lots of preparation for Koloff and Beatrice's big adventure. First, Bobby cleaned out the wagon and put all of Casey's dolls and plastic Smiley Meal Princess Becky toys in a pile. Then he lined the wagon with a bath towel for maximum comfort. Back in his room, it took a while to transfer Beatrice and Koloff into the glass bowl with a fish net.

Bobby carried the bowl with both hands, taking small steps so the water wouldn't spill. Along the way he said in a soothing voice, "Don't worry, guys. I'll take care of you. You're going to have a great time."

Casey filled her empty water cup with dirt and dropped her worm into it as Bobby carefully placed the fishbowl in the wagon. "We'll have to go slow so the water doesn't slosh," he explained to her. "Also, I'll need someone to look out for bumps in the sidewalk so no one gets hurt. Do you know anyone who could do that?"

Casey raised her hand. "I can do that! Bumps," she called out to show him how serious she was. "Bumpitty, bump, bump bump, bump."

Slowly, Bobby pulled the wagon down the block as Casey raced ahead. Every now and then she would shriek, "BUMP!" and he was careful to go around it.

As they made their way through the neighborhood, Bobby pointed out fascinating sights to his passengers. He felt like the guide on the red double-decker bus his family rode when they had taken a tour of Washington, DC.

"And to our left is Holly Harper's house. Beatrice, she's the one who chose you. . . . See that wall over there? That's where I had a huge wipeout when I was first learning to skateboard . . . and that over there is —"

Suddenly Bobby stopped so fast the water in the fishbowl sploshed.

"What?" Casey asked. She was holding a fistful of flowers and a lawn gnome. "What's the matter, Bobby? Did you see a bump?"

Bobby couldn't speak. He couldn't even move. There, planted in front of him on the sidewalk, was the scary cat . . .

the one with twenty-seven toes. It was rumored that the cat was so vicious that it had once destroyed a minivan.

Bobby tried not to look directly at the scary cat for fear that it would lock its eyes on him and then pounce. Instead, he looked up at the sky to show that he wasn't afraid. One could never tell what the scary cat was thinking. That was the problem with sinister beings. They hardly ever told you what they were up to.

"Bobby?" Casey said, peering out from behind him. "He's not going to hurt any of us, is he?"

Bobby had been so afraid the cat was going to attack him that he had forgotten about everyone else. His adrenaline started pumping. He had to get Casey, Beatrice, Koloff, and Wormy Worm Worm out of there. But how? The cat stood firm in the dead center of the sidewalk, as if daring them to pass.

"We'll just have to turn around slowly and go back home," Bobby whispered to Casey. He could see her trembling. "Come on. It's okay. I'll protect you."

As Bobby turned the wagon around, he kept his eyes on the cat, who kept his eyes on him. Every now and then the

cat would release an evil mcow, sending shivers through Bobby.

Slow and steady, slow and steady. Bobby continued down the sidewalk — slow and steady so the water in the fishbowl wouldn't splash.

"Bobby!" Casey gasped. "The cat is following us!"

Sure enough, the scary cat was stalking them. Only now he wasn't looking at Bobby. He was looking at the goldfish.

"Casey," Bobby said, trying to sound braver than he felt. "You pull the wagon with Wormy Worm Worm in it. I'm going to carry Koloff and Beatrice." Casey looked like she was on the verge of tears. "Don't worry," he whispered. "I'm here."

Suddenly, Casey screamed. The cat was now in front of them. "Bobby, do something," she shouted. "He's going to eat us. Do something!"

But what? What could he do? If he could fly, he could whisk them all into the air. If he were invisible, he could push the cat away. If he had superhuman strength, he could pull up the sidewalk. But he was just Bobby.

"Shoo," he said.

The scary cat refused to budge. He just licked his lips and stared at Beatrice and Koloff. Bobby held the fishbowl tighter to his chest. "Shoo!" he said again, trying to sound mean and menacing, only it came out more like a squeak. "Shoo?"

Without warning, something flying as fast as a missile shot out of nowhere and nearly landed on the cat. The cat let out a loud screech and ran away. Bobby looked around to see what had fallen from the sky. Could it have been a meteor?

That's when he saw it.

Of course.

A football.

"Hey, twerps," Annie cried from way down the street. She was on her way home from football practice. "What do you think you're doing?"

"Annie! Annie! Annie!" Casey cried, running into her arms. "That bad cat was going to eat us!"

Annie laughed and hugged Casey. "Well, you're safe now. That cat's not going to bother you as long as I'm around."

Casey hugged her sister harder and buried her face in her football jersey. "Annie, you're our hero! Wait until Mommy and Daddy hear about this!"

"I was going to rescue you," Bobby told Casey.

"I know," she said as she gazed lovingly at her big sister. "But Annie did it first."

CHAPTER 6
Troy Eagle, the Best Athlete

Bobby hated it when they picked teams for soccer in PE. A few kids looked excited, but even more looked distressed, just like he did.

"Since there are twenty-eight of you, we're going to have four teams. That'll make the competition more interesting," Mr. Rainerhaus announced. "Who would like to be a team captain?"

Jillian Zarr's and St. James's hands shot into the air. Another girl and Jackson raised their hands too. "All right, you four. Jillian, you start."

Bobby could tell Holly was disappointed when Jillian Zarr didn't pick her. He felt the same way when neither St. James nor Jackson picked him. As the group of kids who hadn't been picked grew smaller, Bobby shifted from one foot to the other.

When he heard Jackson say, "I'll take Bobby!" his heart lifted.

"Okay, Robert, you're on Jackson's team," Mr. Rainerhaus noted.

Bobby said good-bye to Chess and joined the kids on the other side. When the last kid was picked, he noticed that St. James and Jackson had picked all boys. Jillian Zarr and the other girl picked all girls. This happened every time.

It was Jackson's team against Jillian Zarr's. This made Bobby shudder. The girls were always out to win. The boys got ahead with an early goal, but they didn't hold the lead for long. When one of the girls yelled, "Look, there's a dinosaur!" St. James took his eye off the ball and the girls scored a goal. Then they scored another goal when one of them shouted, "Look, there's a dollar on the ground!"

When the girls won, Bobby couldn't believe how loud and obnoxious they were. Only Holly said to the boys, "Good game." But then Holly was like that. She was the student council representative for Room 15, so it was like her job to be nice to everyone. Bobby was the alternate student council rep, so he didn't have to be quite as nice as Holly, which was a relief because having to be nice all the time would be exhausting.

Still, if his team had won the soccer game, Bobby knew he wouldn't be boastful and rude, like Jillian Zarr. He'd be proud and humble, because though he wasn't good at sports, he knew it was important to be a good sport. His dad always said that.

"Why don't we ever play chess for PE? It's a sport," Chess asked as kids flew past him. Bobby and his buddies were at the new Troy Eagle Skate Park and Rec Center. The great Troy Eagle himself had come to the grand opening, and Bobby had stood in line for two hours to get an auto-graphed poster of the skateboarding superstar.

"I dunno," Bobby answered. He pulled up his kneepads, which had slipped again. Annie always made fun of him for being too skinny. "They ought to have skating in PE. It's a sport. It's part of the X Games. Plus everyone knows Troy Eagle is the best athlete ever."

Over on the far side of the park, two kids had collided and

were both on the ground. Jackson was whooping it up while skating backward. "Look at my fakie!" he yelled. "Look at me!" Chess was a silent skater. He always looked like he was going in slow motion, even when he fell down, which was often. Then there was St. James, who was a daredevil with or without a skateboard. "Everyone, watch me," he yelled seconds before a spectacular crash.

Bobby was a good, solid skater. Not showy, but not a wimp either. He'd study the bigger kids and then start off slow, working his way up to the trick, whether it was as simple as a nosegrind or as hard as an aerial. Though he still had trouble grabbing his board while flying though the air, he was getting better.

One of the things Bobby liked best about skating with his buddies was that no matter what happened, no matter who wiped out, no one was ever made fun of.

Just as he nailed a 360-degree turn, he heard someone yell, "Bobby Bobby Bobby, time to go home!"

Across the skate park, standing outside the fence under the giant Troy Eagle billboard, were Casey and Mr. Ellis-Chan. Both were waving. How long had they been there? He hoped his father had seen his 360.

Bobby nodded to them and glided down the ramp. When he reached the bottom, he slammed the back of his board with his heel so it shot up, then grabbed it midflight and headed toward the gate.

"Quite impressive," Mr. Ellis-Chan said.

Bobby grinned as his dad mussed up his hair.

"We watched you," Casey added. "You're good, Bobby Bobby Bobby! You twirled in the air like a ballerina!"

"That's called a 360," Bobby said. He hoped no one had heard her compare him to a ballerina. "But thanks."

CHAPTER 7
Sandy, Wilbur, and Bobby . . . Arf!

Bobby was having a good time in fourth grade, even if sometimes he got a stomachache from the stress of PE. There were any number of ways he could embarrass himself there, like missing an easy catch during softball, or shooting an air ball in basketball, or playing football. But then, he reasoned, that always made it even nicer to come back to Mrs. Carlson's class. She hardly ever raised her voice; plus she smelled a lot better than Mr. Rainerhaus.

"Class," Mrs. Carlson said. She was wearing Halloween pumpkin earrings. Recently, she had also worn a pair that looked like happy ghosts. "I want you to be silent as we walk to the auditorium. We will be rehearsing the musical on the stage today."

A murmur ran through the room. Up until now they had been practicing on the playground. Even though they weren't doing the entire production of *Annie*, like the professionals did on Broadway, there was still much to learn. Rehearsing on the stage took everything to a whole new level.

As the students walked down the hall in a single-file line, Bobby peered into the classrooms. When he saw Mrs. Woods, his third-grade teacher, he shuddered. One look from her could stop a herd of wild buffalo in its tracks. The second graders were doing math. It looked so easy that Bobby laughed. In the first-grade rooms the kids were making Halloween masks. Bobby couldn't tell what the kindergartners were supposed to be doing — they were all running around the room screaming, except for a boy clutching a bowl of fake fruit and crying in a corner. Casey would be in kindergarten next year.

Mrs. Carlson had her students sit in the audience as she stood on the stage. "We won't be rehearsing our musical from the beginning yet. That will come later. Today we are going to focus on dancing. Please be aware that this stage is not that big. I don't want anyone falling off and getting hurt."

Bobby felt someone poke him. "I'm going to fall off on purpose!" St. James promised.

"Orphans, please," Mrs. Carlson called out. "I need all the orphans and Miss Hannigan onstage now."

Swoozie raised her hand. "Am I an orphan?"

Mrs. Carlson nodded. "Yes, Annie's an orphan."

"Duh," St. James whispered to her. "Little *Orphan* Annie. Orphan. Annie. Orphan. Duh."

Swoozie ignored him. The girls were experts at ignoring St. James.

Bobby and St. James sat back and relaxed. Daddy Warbucks and Sandy weren't in this scene. It looked like a lot of fun dancing on the stage, and even Jackson and Chess were laughing. Some of the girls were really good dancers, including Holly, who had studied at Mrs. Cusak's School of Ballet and Tap for three years. When they were little, Bobby and Holly had taken Mrs. Cusak's Bitsy Baby Bounce-Bounce class together, and Bobby had won the Itsy-Bitsy Bouncer Award. He hoped that Holly would never ever tell anyone about this.

Finally, it was time for Annie, Sandy, and Daddy Warbucks to practice their big number. It was exciting standing on the stage. The kids sitting in the audience looked so small. As Swoozie and St. James tried out their dance, Bobby ran around on all fours barking. It felt great making everyone laugh.

"Sandy! Sandy, be careful not to trip Annie or Daddy Warbucks," Mrs. Carlson cautioned him. "Daddy Warbucks,

you're looking a little stiff. Can you loosen up a bit? Annie, you're doing a wonderful job, but make sure you don't step on Sandy."

Dancing and dog romping were way more complicated than they looked, Bobby learned. Before he could try out his barking again, the rehearsal ended.

"Tomorrow we'll put the songs and the dances together. That's when this will really start turning into a musical," Mrs. Carlson said enthusiastically. "Now, here are letters to your parents. Each of you will be responsible for your own costumes. If you can't bring one in, talk to me privately about it and I'll make sure you get whatever you need."

Bobby looked at his letter. It read:

Dear Parents,
BOBBY has been selected to play *SANDY* in our class production of *Annie*. Please provide a *DOG COSTUME* for your child. We look forward to seeing you at the musical on Thursday, October 29th at 7 p.m.
Yours truly,
Mrs. Carlson

On the bottom of the letter, Mrs. Carlson had added in her neat cursive, *P.S. Bobby is doing an excellent job as Sandy!*

Bobby read the letter a couple of times. He was proud to have been selected to play Sandy, and was determined to be the best Sandy ever.

"Wilbur could be Sandy," Chess mused as they walked home after school. Wilbur was Chess's dog and the finest canine Bobby had ever met, even if his breath smelled like sneakers and his fur was always matted in odd patches. They stopped at the ice-cream truck. Chess bought a strawberry Popsicle and Bobby dug around his pockets for quarters to buy his usual AstroPop. "Sandy's a mutt and Wilbur's a mutt," Chess continued as he unwrapped his Popsicle.

Bobby nodded. That was true. He hoped Chess wouldn't mention this to Mrs. Carlson or else he might be replaced. However, he thought it would be totally cool to have a real dog onstage.

"Hey, Chess," Bobby said, "can I come over and watch Wilbur? You know, to see how he walks and runs. It's research."

"Sure," said Chess. "But don't touch Wilbur. Remember what happened last time."

How could Bobby forget? He had given Wilbur a huge hug and that triggered a particularly bad asthma attack. Still, he loved dogs, so it had been worth it.

Bobby knew that famous actors always researched their roles. His sister Annie had told him that when Mike Marvel played the rugged surfer spy in the movie *Missiles Over Maui*, he had eaten nothing but coconuts for a month to prepare for the role.

Dog biscuits didn't taste any worse than his dad's home-made cookies. Bobby knew this for a fact. Maybe he'd eat dog biscuits the week before the show, or at least the night of it.

Bobby perched on the front porch and watched Chess and Wilbur run around. One of Wilbur's legs was shorter than the others. Bobby wondered if all of Sandy's legs were the same length, and how he'd find out something like that. He wanted to get the part exactly right. To make sure he wouldn't forget anything, Bobby drew pictures on the back of his math work-sheet. Pictures of Wilbur running. Wilbur standing. Wilbur sitting. Wilbur happy. Wilbur sad.

Wilbur drooled a lot, so Bobby tried drooling like the dog, but quickly ran out of spit. Later, he decided it was best not to drool onstage because someone might slip, and Mrs. Carlson had specifically said that she didn't want anyone falling off the stage.

When it was time to go home, Bobby held off the urge to hug Wilbur. "Thanks for everything," he told the mutt. Then, in Sandy speak, Bobby added, "Arf, arf . . . aaaaarf!!!"

"ARF!!!" Wilbur answered.

CHAPTER 8
Sew What

Bobby lay upside down on the couch and watched *Princess Becky's Planet* with Casey. Da-Da-Doo, the pint-sized dragon, was delivering a letter to the Terrible Teeny Tiny Trolls. That's when Bobby suddenly remembered his letter about the Sandy costume. When he emptied his backpack, there was a trio of craggy rocks, part of his lunch from last week, and a bunch of crumpled papers. He found the letter and held it out to his dad.

Mr. Ellis-Chan stopped dusting and sat down to read. "It looks like we're supposed to supply your costume for the class musical."

"I'm the dog, Sandy," Bobby said proudly. To show what a great Sandy he was going to be, he began to bark and romp around the room on all fours. Casey joined him.

"Really? Sandy the dog? I didn't know that," his dad

replied, even though Bobby had told him this before. "Well, I'll get started on your dog costume right away. I've always wanted to try my hand at sewing!"

Bobby froze midbark. "Dad, can't we just buy a costume?"

"Why bother to buy one?" Mr. Ellis-Chan said. He flexed his massive biceps, which, Bobby knew, helped his father think. "We have Grammy's old sewing machine in the attic. Bobby, I am going to make you the best darn dog costume in the world!"

Casey wrinkled her nose. "I didn't know Daddy could sew," she said as Mr. Ellis-Chan ran upstairs.

Bobby picked up Mrs. Carlson's letter off the floor. "I'm not so sure he can," he said solemnly.

After a dinner of Mr. Ellis-Chan's tuna casserole soup, Mrs. Ellis-Chan took the family to Burger Barn for a snack. Then they headed to Sew What, the fabric store.

Bobby had never been to a fabric store before. There were aisles dedicated to all sorts of yarn: thick, thin, fluffy, and fuzzy. Spools of thread in every color imaginable, even cerulean, took up an entire wall. And the knitting needles looked like the kinds of weapons that Mike Marvel, the action hero, might use when fighting off surfer spies.

As Bobby explored the store, he wished he had his skateboard. It would have been so cool to skate through Sew What, making sharp cuts around the end displays and running his hand over the rows and rows of colorful material.

"Can we go now?" Annie moaned. "I don't even know why I'm here!"

"How about this?" his mother said, pulling out a nice yellowish cotton fabric.

"I think Sandy is more sandy colored," Bobby noted. He was staring at some black material with glow-in-the-dark planets on it. It seemed like that would be good for something. Maybe he could talk his mother into using it for new curtains in the living room.

"What about this?" Casey said, tugging on a bolt of fabric. It was pink and purple with hearts on it.

"Can we go now?" Annie said louder, this time with an exaggerated yawn.

Bobby wondered if all teenagers were like Annie, or if her moodiness was unique. He had asked her about it once, but after she screamed, "I AM NOT MOODY!" he thought it best not to bring it up anymore.

"Well, Bobby, what do you think of Casey's fabric selection?" his mother asked, smiling.

He smiled back, then said to Casey, "That's nice, but not quite right for a dog costume."

"Can we go now?" Annie asked. "When can we go? Hello? Is anyone listening to me?"

"Annie, I told you, we'll leave once Bobby finds what he's looking for," Mrs. Ellis-Chan said patiently.

"Hurry up, slowpoke," Annie hissed to her brother.

Suddenly, a voice boomed, "I FOUND IT!" At first Bobby thought the store's loudspeaker was on, then he recognized his father's voice. "Bobby, get over to the Halloween create-a-costume aisle."

Bobby rushed over to aisle number thirteen. His father

was beaming and soon Bobby was too. Mr. Ellis-Chan held a bolt of fabric over his head as if he were lifting weights. It was exactly what Bobby was looking for. The fabric looked like real fur. It was light brown, and fuzzy, and perfect!

As soon as they got home, Mr. Ellis-Chan set up the sewing machine in the guest room where Grammy and Gramps stayed when they visited.

"Wow, it's pretty," Casey said as she ran her hands over it.

"Be careful," Mrs. Ellis-Chan warned. "The needle is sharp."

"I know!" Casey said, nodding. "Snow White pricked her finger on a sewing machine and fell into a deep sleep until the Frog Prince saved her by giving her shoes that fit."

"Casey, it was Sleeping Beauty, and she pricked her finger on a spinning wheel," Bobby informed her. They had studied fairy tales in the second grade.

"Maybe, maybe not," Casey said. "But I like my story better. Daddy," she asked, "how does the sewing machine work?"

Mr. Ellis-Chan shrugged. "I'm not sure. But how hard can it be?"

CHAPTER 9
Football Stress

Luckily for Bobby, he didn't have PE every day. It was Monday, Wednesday, and Friday, leaving him Tuesday and Thursday, plus the weekend, to recover. Mr. Rainerhaus was a very stern teacher. Each class started with fifty jumping jacks and a brisk run around the playground with him yelling, "Faster! Go faster!"

Bobby didn't like it when people yelled at him. Some kids didn't let it bother them when they were yelled at, like St. James. St. James got yelled at all the time. But when someone yelled at Bobby, even if it was a despicable person like Jillian Zarr, it made him feel bad for a long time.

"Forty-seven, forty-eight, forty-nine, fifty!"

Mr. Rainerhaus blew his whistle. Everyone stopped, except for Jackson. Jackson was weird and loved jumping jacks as much as Bobby loved skateboarding. If there was a world record for jumping jacks, Jackson could probably break it. Bobby wondered if one day he'd ever break any records, like Troy Eagle. Troy held the world-record ollie — fifty-two inches in the air. That was taller than Bobby.

"I know we've been playing soccer for a while," Mr. Rainerhaus announced, "so it's time for a change. And this one will be quite a treat! We'll finish up soccer today and start a new sport on Monday."

Bobby blinked several times. It looked like Mr. Rainerhaus was smiling at him.

"What do you think we'll play next?" Chess whispered.

Bobby shrugged. He was fine with soccer. Soccer wasn't so bad. All you had to do was run up and down the field. He could do that. During the last game, he scored a point when Swoozie, who was the goalie, was watching a butterfly.

Bobby hoped they wouldn't be playing softball. Softball was bad news. You could get hit by the ball and get a concussion. His dad had gotten a concussion more than once when playing football.

At the end of soccer, Mr. Rainerhaus gathered the students. "We have a celebrity among us!" he announced. Bobby tried to spot the celebrity, but all he saw was one of the boys picking his nose by pretending he had an itch, and a girl scratching her armpit and then looking horrified when she saw Bobby watching. Maybe Swoozie was the celebrity because she was such a good singer.

Then Mr. Rainerhaus winked at Bobby and proclaimed, "I can't believe I've gone all this time without realizing that the son of my all-time favorite football player is in this class!"

Bobby flinched.

"Bobby Ellis-Chan, why didn't you tell me that The Freezer is your father?" Mr. Rainerhaus squatted, put one arm out, and growled in an imitation of The Freezer's most famous move. "Best linebacker the LA Earthquakes ever had. Best darn football player this country has ever seen!" Mr. Rainerhaus enthused. "My world stood still when Sam Benzoni tackled The Freezer and busted his knee. The day he retired from football was one of the saddest days of my life. I even cried. And I'm man enough to admit that!"

He looked like he was about to cry again.

Bobby decided to change his superhero power from superhuman strength to invisibility. He would give anything to be invisible right now.

"So!" Mr. Rainerhaus said, clearing his throat, "in honor of The Freezer, and because we have his very own son right here in this class, next week we will start — FOOTBALL! Bobby Ellis-Chan, I'm going to be watching you," he said, wagging a finger at Bobby. "I'll bet you can teach this class a thing or two. Heck, I'll bet you could teach *me*. Perhaps," Mr. Rainerhaus laughed, "I'll just have you take over."

Bobby glanced at Holly. She looked as worried as he did.

"Okay then," Mr. Rainerhaus called out. "Class dismissed!"

Before Bobby could make his way back to Room 15, Mr. Rainerhaus stopped him. "It really is an honor to be your teacher," he said. Then he shook Bobby's hand so hard it made Bobby's head bobble up and down. "I wonder . . ." Mr. Rainerhaus hesitated. "Is there any way I could meet your dad? Maybe he could come to PE. It would mean so much to me."

"I'll see what I can do," Bobby mumbled. He flexed his fingers to see if they still worked. "But my dad's pretty busy, you know, with stuff and things and stuff and . . . um, stuff. So he probably can't come to school."

Mr. Rainerhaus grew solemn. "I understand," he said, nodding. "A man like The Freezer probably has lots of important things to do."

CHAPTER 10
Fish Tank Talk

When Bobby got home, he found his father unsuccessfully trying to remove the living room curtains from the vacuum cleaner. Bobby was feeling on edge. It was like that queasy feeling he got when watching scary movies with Annie — he knew something bad was going to happen, but he didn't know when. Except that Bobby knew he was doomed next Monday at 10 A.M. during PE.

After greeting his dad, Bobby ditched his backpack in favor of his board and skated up and down his street. With each shuv-it, as he spun his skateboard 180 degrees, he loosened up. There was something liberating about skating. Planting your feet on the deck and the feeling of the sidewalk beneath you. The freedom of flight when you got air, and the hard solid landings when you ollied just right. Getting speed and then cruising. With skating, it was just Bobby and his board. No teams. No teacher. No rules.

Casey was squealing as she ran around the front lawn and pretended the lawn gnome was chasing her. "Gnomey Gnome Gnome was abandoned and I rescued him," she had told her mother. "You said you wanted something for the garden, and he's practically as good as a moat!"

"Hey, Bobby, can I try?"

Bobby was surprised to see his father watching him from the driveway. "Oh, uh, sure," he told his dad. "You'll need a brain bucket, though." Mr. Ellis-Chan looked at him blankly. "A brain bucket is a helmet," Bobby explained.

"How's this?" his father said, returning with his LA Earthquakes football helmet.

Bobby nodded. "That'll do."

When his dad stepped on the skateboard and it bowed in the middle, Bobby grimaced. That was the board that Grammy and Gramps had let him pick out over the summer — the new Troy Eagle Pro 99 deck with Eagle trucks and Greased Lightning smooth-action titanium bearings. "Wait!" Bobby shouted. He ran into the house and brought out his old Troy Eagle Super 74 board. It was worn in all the right places from grinding the axles on the curb, the nose was battered from tricks, and there were Go Girly Girl stickers all over it courtesy of Casey, but otherwise it was in great shape.

"Here, use this," Bobby said, offering up his old skateboard.

Mr. Ellis-Chan leapt on the board, then slowly he pushed off and headed down the street, gaining speed until . . .

CRASH!

"Are you okay?" Bobby yelled, running to his father.

"Wipeout!" Casey cried, hopping up and down and clapping. "Daddy wiped out! I'll get my doctor's kit."

Mr. Ellis-Chan looked stricken as he got up. Bobby stared at the skateboard. It had snapped in half.

"I owe you one," his father finally said. "I'm sorry, Bobby."

Bobby clutched his broken skateboard. That was the board he had learned kick turns on. He wanted to cry, but held back. "That's okay, Dad," he said. "I've got my new board."

"But I broke it. I should have known better."

"Really, it's okay," Bobby insisted.

"Guess I should just stick to football," his dad mumbled. "I'm no Troy Eagle. Well, I'd better go start dinner."

Bobby stood holding his broken board as he watched his father trudge down the street toward home.

Later, while his father was downstairs in the kitchen stirring a big pot of something orange, Bobby checked in on Koloff and Beatrice. They looked bored. "Here," he said, nudging the soccer ball with his finger. "Try pushing the ball."

Neither appeared interested.

Rover could push his soccer ball into a net, and maneuver in and out of the hoops. Rover could follow Bobby's hand signals to swim back and forth, and even do flips. Even though it had been nearly a month since Rover died, Bobby still thought about him every day. Sometimes he would go into the backyard where Rover was buried and leave little presents, like a shiny penny or an interesting rock. He missed talking to him. Rover had been an excellent listener.

"Hey, you guys," Bobby said as Beatrice circled the castle. "Do you have a couple of minutes to chat?" When they didn't say no, Bobby took that as a sign that he should continue. "My PE teacher thinks that just because I'm The Freezer's son, I'm good at football. I've got until Monday to figure out what to do."

Koloff and Beatrice were silent for the longest time.

"I know," Bobby agreed. "This is a tough one. I'm eating seven meals a day, and I'm doing a hundred sit-ups and push-ups every morning. Well, starting tomorrow I'm going to do that. I figure, if I'm bigger and stronger, I'll be better at football and won't embarrass myself in front of Mr. Rainerhaus and my class."

Koloff did a spin around the aquarium.

"What was that?" Bobby asked. He sensed that Koloff was trying to tell him something. But he couldn't figure out what the fish wanted him to know. "What is it, Koloff? Is it about football?"

Koloff swam around the tank again.

"Something about not embarrassing myself?"

When Koloff rested inside the castle, Bobby gave up trying to guess what his fish was trying to tell him. Koloff wasn't like Rover, who was easy to understand. "Well, okay then, thanks for listening. We can talk more later. In the meantime, look what I have for you!" Bobby brought out one of the hoops that Rover used to play with. Carefully, he placed it in the water.

"Hey, squirt!" It was Annie. Her football jersey was covered in dirt. She looked into the aquarium. Koloff stared back at her. "What's up?"

"Not much."

"Well, guess what?" Annie said. Even though she was wearing her helmet, Bobby could see her smile. "Coach says I'm one of the best quarterbacks Rancho Rosetta High School has ever had. Can you believe that?"

"I can believe that," Bobby said. His voice was flat.

"You don't sound too happy," Annie said. "What's with you?"

"What's with *you*?" Bobby shot back. "Why do you have to be so good at football?"

"Whoa, what's your problem?"

Bobby stared at Diver Dave. "I don't have a problem," he said as his jaw tensed. "Everything's fine. Now leave me alone."

"Geez," Annie muttered as she backed out of the room. "And you say that *I'm* moody!"

Bobby waited until he was sure she was gone to start talking to his fish again. "It's not fair," he told them. "I'll never be like Annie, no matter how hard I try."

CHAPTER 11
Big and Strong?

All weekend the familiar sound of the sewing machine whirring away filled the air. To Bobby, it seemed like his dad had been working on the Sandy costume forever. Yet whenever he'd ask about it, Mr. Ellis-Chan would say, "Soon enough, son. You'll have to wait until it's done to get the full effect!"

While Annie was out buying Halloween decorations with Mrs. Ellis-Chan, Casey stayed home to watch *Princess Becky's Planet*. Princess Becky sang to the Halloween pumpkins to make them grow big and strong. *That's what I need*, Bobby thought. *If I could get Princess Becky to sing to me, maybe I'd get big and strong.*

As he watched the rest of the show, Bobby wondered if his mom would let him quit school. He didn't want to face Mr. Rainerhaus on Monday. Perhaps he could get a job. Bobby tried to think of what he was qualified to do. Ice-cream tester. Donut taster. Rock collector.

The sewing machine noise ceased and Mr. Ellis-Chan appeared in the doorway holding a football. "Bobby, how about tossing the ball with me for a bit?"

Normally when his dad asked him to play football, Bobby said no. But this time was different. Maybe, just maybe, a miracle would occur and he could learn enough not to humiliate himself during PE. It was a long shot, but anything was worth trying.

"Sure, Dad, why not?"

Mr. Ellis-Chan lit up. "Really? Wow! All right then, let's go!"

The targets and other things were still set up for Annie's football drills, but Bobby was more interested in just throwing the ball and catching it. He knew the rules of the game pretty well. Bobby had watched football lots of times on TV with his father. Whenever someone got tackled, Bobby shut his eyes. He didn't like seeing people get hurt.

The last time his dad played professionally, Bobby had been six years old. When The Freezer got knocked down and didn't get up, both Bobby and his mother started crying.

Later, at the hospital, Bobby was still crying. He thought his father was going to die. But he didn't die. Instead, his knee was so busted that he would never play pro ball again. Bobby never told his dad, but he was happy when he heard the news. That meant he wouldn't get hurt anymore. Only, these days Annie was playing football and now Bobby worried about her, even though she was tougher than most boys.

Mr. Ellis-Chan lined up five footballs on the ground in front of him. "First, we'll practice catching. I'll throw these to you one after the other. You just catch the ball, then drop it and catch the next one, okay?"

Bobby felt his body tense as he nodded. Five footballs meant that he could mess up five times in a row.

"It might help if you open your eyes when I throw the ball to you," Mr. Ellis-Chan suggested.

Bobby did his best to keep his eyes open as his father threw. Still, he missed almost every time. Once he did catch the ball, but it hurt when the pointy part hit his chest. *Why don't they make footballs softer?* he wondered.

They switched to throwing. "Okay, hold the ball like this," his father said, showing Bobby what to do.

Bobby tried to imitate his dad, but the ball was too big for his hands. Plus, it never went very far when he threw it, and it certainly didn't have that same spin The Freezer's or Annie's throws had.

"You just need more upper-body strength," Mr. Ellis-Chan was saying. "Put more muscle into your throw, like this." Effortlessly, the football sailed across the sky. "You'll get there. Don't worry."

But Bobby did worry. He had to get there by Monday.

★ ★ ★

That night before bed, Mrs. Ellis-Chan came in to check on her son. "New poster?" she asked.

Bobby nodded. He had just put up his autographed Troy Eagle poster on his wall — the one of Troy doing an aerial over the Grand Canyon.

"What shall we talk about tonight, Bobby?" his mother asked as she fluffed up his pillow and motioned for him to get into bed. As was their custom, they had a nightly talk about the universe, or rocks, or skateboarding. It was Bobby's job to decide, and he always picked interesting subjects.

"Mom," he began, "when do you think I'll start growing?" He had been thinking about this a lot lately.

Mrs. Ellis-Chan took Bobby's hand in hers. "Well, I can feel you growing right now!" she exclaimed.

Bobby took his hand back. "No, really, Mom. I'm serious."

His mother brushed the hair away from his eyes. "Yes, I can tell you are, and that you're not a little kid anymore." Bobby nodded. He was happy his mother had noticed. "Everyone gets their growth spurts at different times. You'll have yours soon enough. How tall are you compared to the other kids in your grade?"

"Not the smallest, but nowhere near the tallest," he said. "Do you ever think I'll ever be as big as Dad?"

"Hmmm," his mother mused. "That's unlikely, because you're a combination of my side of the family and his. If you think about it, your father is way bigger than either of his parents were. As for his strength, you know how much your father works out."

Bobby nodded. His dad was always lifting weights in the garage, and he ran a couple miles a day with Annie. Sometimes Bobby followed them on his bike.

"Annie's pretty tall," he pointed out.

"Yes, and Annie is in high school. But by the time you're her age, you will be a lot taller, I promise," his mother reassured him. "Any other questions? Or are you stalling for time now?"

Bobby started to say something, but then stopped himself. "All done," he said.

His mother kissed him on the forehead. "Okay then! Now, lights out. It's time for bed. Getting plenty of sleep will help you grow! Good night, honey."

"Good night, Mom."

Bobby did have one more question, but it always got stuck in his throat. He wanted to know what "He's not like me" meant.

CHAPTER 12
A Room Full of Fears

On Monday morning, Mrs. Carlson announced, "Class, Mr. Rainerhaus has food poisoning and is out sick today, so PE is canceled."

Bobby tried not to grin, because that would be rude. Still, he felt a wave of relief wash over him. No PE! No football! But when he turned toward Chess, it looked like Chess had food poisoning too.

"Are you okay?" Bobby asked.

"I'm nervous," Chess croaked.

"What are you nervous about?"

"About the musical. My uncle Carrom is coming, and he's a great singer," Chess explained. "Every family reunion, he forces us to listen as he sings Bollywood songs. He says he's bringing all the relatives to the musical — and you know how many of those I have."

"Well, I'm scared I'm going to forget my lines," St. James confessed. "I had no idea Daddy Warbucks was such a blabbermouth."

"Boys," Mrs. Carlson said, "is there something you'd like to share with the class?"

St. James pointed to Chess. "He's scared."

"So is he!" Chess cried, pointing back at St. James.

Mrs. Carlson looked curious. "What exactly scares the two of you?"

"The musical," Chess said softly.

Several students nodded in agreement.

"Well," Mrs. Carlson said, "let's take a few minutes to talk about our fears. It's an excellent subject." Chess sat up straighter. So did St. James. "What are the kinds of things that you find scary? I know that when I was your age, I was scared of the dark, and to this day I still sleep with a night-light on."

Bobby was happy to hear that his teacher had a night-light too.

Everyone had their hands raised, ready to share what scared them.

"Wow, this is certainly a hot topic," Mrs. Carlson noted. "I think we're going to need to spend more than a few minutes on this. Okay, here's what we are going to do. I'd like everyone to write down what scares you. You don't need to include your names. Then I'll write everyone's fears on the board and we can talk about them. If you don't want to write anything, you don't have to."

Some students began writing immediately. Others stared off into the distance. A few chewed on their pencils or fingernails. Bobby disguised his handwriting by slanting the letters to the left.

After about ten minutes, Mrs. Carlson asked the class to fold their papers in half and pass them forward. "After recess we'll talk about this," she said. "In the meantime, please take out your history books."

Later, as the boys waited for their turns at the handball court, Jackson asked Bobby, "What are you afraid of?"

Bobby just shrugged. "Things," he said. "What about you?"

Jackson shrugged. "Same as you. Things."

When the class returned from recess, the blackboard was filled with fears. Bobby was surprised to see so many. Mrs. Carlson had written . . .

And the list went on.

"I think it's great that you were able to identify your fears," Mrs. Carlson told the class. "These are all very real and very valid worries. So many times there are things we are afraid of, but we don't talk about them, and that could actually make it seem worse. Some of these fears you can do something about. Others, you may just have to face.

"For example, I know that many of you are nervous about the musical. Singing and dancing in front of a lot of people can be frightening. But the more you practice, the easier it will be. I've also heard that if you imagine everyone in the audience is just wearing their underwear, they won't seem so scary."

Bobby and the rest of the class howled with laughter. It was funny to hear a teacher say "underwear," and imagining a room full of people in their underwear was even funnier.

Mrs. Carlson continued, "If you're worried about global warming, then maybe you can help try to stop it. You may not be able to do this single-handedly, but just knowing that you are part of the solution may make you feel better. Does anyone else have some ideas on how to cope with any of these fears? You don't have to say which one is yours."

Jillian Zarr raised her hand. "If you are afraid of clowns, then don't go to the circus."

"That's good thinking," Mrs. Carlson said. She pointed to Swoozie next.

"If you don't want to go to Principal Coun's office, then you shouldn't do anything bad," Swoozie said, looking at St. James. "Oh, and I'm scared of robbers. One of our lawn gnomes was stolen a couple weeks ago, and in the middle of the day too!"

Bobby's eyes grew big when he heard this.

"You should carry a dart gun and a cage to capture the small animals with sharp teeth," Jackson said. "Plus always bring bait, like a pepperoni pizza."

As the class discussed everyone's fears, Bobby waited for someone to come up with a solution to his. But nobody did.

"And so, remember," Mrs. Carlson said at last. "Talk to someone about your worries. Don't let them grow inside of you. Find someone you trust and share how you feel. You'd be surprised at how just talking can make you feel better."

CHAPTER 13
A Regular Person

Casey whacked her brother over the head with Wandee II, her new wand. "Bobby, wake up!"

Bobby groaned and buried himself deeper under his covers. Was it Wednesday already? Mr. Rainerhaus had probably recovered from his food poisoning, and that meant there would be PE today. Maybe it would be best just to stay in bed and avoid Wednesday altogether.

After a while it grew quiet. *Good*, Bobby thought, *Casey has left*. It was getting stuffy under the covers. But when he came up for air . . . SPLASH!

"Casey!" Bobby yelled. "Why did you do that?"

"Do what?" Casey smiled sweetly as she tried to hide an empty water glass behind her back. "Mommy told me to wake you up. Now get up, Bobby Bobby Bobby!!!"

"Hey, sleepyhead," Mrs. Ellis-Chan said when Bobby finally made it downstairs to breakfast. "Since when did you start taking showers in the morning?"

"I didn't take a shower," Bobby growled. "It was raining in my room."

Casey giggled.

"Got some cream-of-wheat waffles for you right here," his father said, placing a plate of charred blobs in front of him.

Bobby glanced at Annie, who was shaking her head and mouthing, "Don't eat them." She was wearing her football helmet and a jersey. He used to wonder why she wore it every day. Now Bobby realized why. If he could play football as well as Annie, he'd do the same thing so everyone would know that he was important. At her last football game, the entire Ellis-Chan family sat in the bleachers and cheered as Bobby's big sister completed pass after pass.

"Eat up, Annie," her father said, refilling her glass with milk. "You want to bulk up for your game on Friday. When the other team sees you out there passing the ball, they'll wish they never heard of the Rancho Rosetta High School Tigers!"

On the walk to school, Bobby was unusually quiet.

"What are you thinking about?" Holly asked. She offered him half of her Toasty Oatsie cereal bar.

"Nothing," he said as he munched.

"Worried about Mr. Rainerhaus?"

"Yeah," Bobby admitted.

"Is your dad coming to school?"

"I didn't even tell him about Mr. Rainerhaus," Bobby said. "He'd probably get all upset to learn we're playing football during PE. My dad knows what a loser I am."

They silently picked up their pace when they passed the house where the scary cat lived. Cobwebs crowded the windows and the creaky wooden gate was falling apart. Paint peeled off the sides of the house. It seemed ready for Halloween, except that it always looked like that.

"I can't imagine your dad calling you a loser," Holly said once they cleared the Halloween house.

"He doesn't have to say it," Bobby replied glumly. "I just know it."

For once Bobby wished the clock would slow down. He was dreading PE more than he ever dreaded anything in his life.

During silent study, Bobby made up a list of things he would rather do than face Mr. Rainerhaus.

1. Go to the dentist
2. Eat a bug
3. Be friends with Jillian Zarr
4. Get a Mohawk

Then he crossed out #3 and replaced it with *Clean the attic*.

When the dreaded hour for PE finally arrived, Mr. Rainerhaus beamed at him with such intensity that Bobby was momentarily blinded. "Bobby Ellis-Chan, come up front with me," his teacher instructed. Reluctantly, Bobby did as he was told. "Is your father coming today?"

"Not today," Bobby answered. His throat was dry.

"Well, maybe another day," Mr. Rainerhaus said, trying not to look disappointed. He faced the class. "Today we start football, and I'm honored that Bobby has agreed to be my assistant!"

Bobby shook his head. He hadn't agreed to help.

Some of the girls snickered.

"First we'll break into four teams. Bobby, it seems only right that you be a team captain. Volunteers for the other captains?"

As usual, Jillian Zarr, Jackson, and St. James raised their hands.

"All righty! Let's begin. Bobby, you pick first," Mr. Rainerhaus instructed.

Bobby had never been a team captain before. Some kids looked directly at him. Others waved. A few jumped up and down. Chess held his hands up as if pleading and gave Bobby the same wide-eyed look Wilbur used when he wanted another dog biscuit.

"Chess Kapur," Bobby said.

Chess grinned so wide that it took up half his face. As he stepped behind Bobby he whispered, "Thank you, thank you, thank you."

As Bobby expected, Jillian, Jackson, and St. James picked the most athletic kids. When it was Bobby's turn to pick again, he called out, "Holly Harper."

A murmur ran through the class. A girl had never been on a team with the boys before. But the way Bobby figured it, since there were three boy team captains and one girl team captain, some girls would have to be with boys anyway. Holly high-fived with Chess as she took her place behind Bobby. When the last person was called, Bobby's team included Chess, Holly, Swoozie, Amy and Amelia (two girls Bobby always had trouble telling apart), and Kip, a boy who was semi-famous because in second grade he had broken both wrists in a freak bowling accident.

Once the teams were decided, Mr. Rainerhaus tossed

footballs to each team captain. Bobby caught his and looked around to see if anyone had noticed. "Let's begin with the basics," Mr. Rainerhaus shouted.

Everyone took turns holding the ball. At least Bobby knew how to do that. When it came time to throw, Jillian Zarr's ball spiraled way past the tetherball courts. St. James and Jackson were pretty good at throwing too. Swoozie's ball somehow went straight up, and Chess's ball hit Holly in the knee.

Then it was Bobby's turn.

"Okay, everyone, gather around," Mr. Rainerhaus said. "I want you all to see this."

Bobby felt his chest tighten. Was he having a heart attack? What if he collapsed right now? He felt like throwing up. That was a sure pass out of PE. Maybe if he had a heart attack, threw up, *and* broke both wrists, he could get out of PE for the rest of the year.

Mr. Rainerhaus handed Bobby a football. "Show these kids how to throw. I'll go long and you pass it to me."

Bobby watched in silent panic as Mr. Rainerhaus jogged to the far side of the playground. He looked like a speck.

Bobby realized that if he turned around and ran home right now, Mr. Rainerhaus would have a hard time catching up to him.

"Any time now," Mr. Rainerhaus shouted. "I'm ready."

Bobby motioned for Mr. Rainerhaus to come closer. Then closer. Then closer still, until he was about five feet from him. Bobby tossed him the ball.

"What was *that*?" Jillian Zarr asked. "Are you playing hot potato?"

Mr. Rainerhaus shook his head. "I'm disappointed," he said.

Even though Bobby was standing still, his heart was racing. He was glad his father wasn't there to see this.

"Bobby, it was unfair of me to ask you to show off in front of everyone," he heard Mr. Rainerhaus say. "We all know that if you're one-tenth the athlete your father is, you could make that ball sail over the school into the street. Yet you chose not to show off. That's the sign of a true gentleman."

St. James started to say something, but stopped when Holly pinched him.

Bobby didn't think it was possible, but now he felt even worse. Mr. Rainerhaus had gotten it all wrong. He wasn't one-tenth the athlete his dad was. He wasn't even one-one-hundredth.

The class dragged on. Bobby's team was as bad as he thought they'd be. At one point, both Chess and Bobby fell down when they ran into each other. And when Holly scored a touchdown — for the opposing team — she looked like she was going to cry.

By the time the class was over, Bobby was ready to hide under a rock. But Mr. Rainerhaus had other plans. "Bobby," he said. "Stay behind and help me."

In silence, Bobby and Mr. Rainerhaus returned the football equipment to the PE shed. Finally Bobby spoke up. "Mr. Rainerhaus, I'm sorry I'm so lousy at football. I can't even throw."

Mr. Rainerhaus smiled at Bobby. He didn't look nearly as scary when he smiled. "You can throw," he said. "Well, okay, so maybe when you throw, your ball doesn't go as far as you'd like . . . or even in the right direction, but you can throw. In fact, I was quite impressed when you threw the ball and it spiraled behind you. I've never seen that before. Listen, Bobby, if you just practice, you can probably get a lot better. I'm sure your dad can help you get really good at football."

"But what if I don't want to play football?" Bobby blurted out angrily. "Do I have to just because my dad did?" He covered his mouth. Bobby had never said that out loud before.

"You have a good point," Mr. Rainerhaus said slowly. He sat down on the bench and motioned for Bobby to sit too. "My father wanted me to be a doctor, like him. I even started to study medicine until I realized that being a doctor wasn't who I was meant to be."

Bobby nodded. Mr. Rainerhaus knew how he felt.

"I'm sorry I put you on the spot," his teacher continued. "I was so thrilled to learn who your father is that I mistook you for him."

Hearing this made Bobby laugh. No one had ever mistaken him for The Freezer before. "Thanks, Mr. Rainerhaus," Bobby said. "That's a first!"

As Mr. Rainerhaus walked him back to Room 15, Bobby thought that maybe Mr. Rainerhaus wasn't so awful once you got to know him. In fact, he no longer seemed like a mean PE teacher. Instead, Mr. Rainerhaus almost seemed like a regular person.

CHAPTER 14

Dress Rehearsal

And bring your costumes tomorrow," Mrs. Carlson reminded the class. "We will be having our one and only dress rehearsal."

St. James hoisted his backpack over his shoulder. "You should see my Daddy Warbucks costume," he bragged. "It's got shoulder pads and everything. I look so good!"

Bobby zipped his Troy Eagle backpack shut. His father had been working on his costume forever, but he refused to let anyone see it. Bobby wasn't sure what to expect, especially since his dad had never sewn anything before, unless you counted an upside-down patch on Annie's letterman's jacket.

That afternoon, when Bobby got home, Casey and Wormy Worm Worm greeted him. "You should be more careful," Bobby advised his sister as she dangled her worm in his face. "I'm not sure if Wormy likes that."

"Oh!" Casey gently kissed her worm, then placed him back in the dirt patch. "Bobby, want to play? Pleeeeease!!!"

Bobby had homework, plus he needed to check on his Sandy costume. But when he looked at Casey, who had her eyes screwed shut and her fingers crossed, he said, "Okay, but just for half an hour. I have important things to do."

"Will I have important things to do when I'm big like you, Bobby?" Casey asked as she followed him into the house.

He nodded. "Sure. In fact, you already do a lot of important things."

Casey's jaw dropped. "I do? Like what? Tell me!"

"Well, you take good care of Wormy Worm Worm," Bobby said. Casey nodded. "And you always make sure your crown is on straight."

Casey touched her crown. "Princess Becky says that a true princess always wears her crown with pride. What else, Bobby? What other important things do I do?"

He gave it some thought. "Well, Mom always asks you to wake me up in the morning so I'm not late to school. And if you didn't do that, and I was late every day, then I might get kicked out of the fourth grade. And if that happened, I couldn't get into fifth grade or any other grade, and I might end up a ne'er-do-well."

"Bobby," his little sister asked, "what's a ne'er-do-well?"

"I'm not sure," he answered. "I heard it on the *Hop-a-long Howdy Cowboy Show*, and I don't think it's a good thing."

Casey's eyes welled up with tears. "I don't want you to become a ne'er-do-well," she sobbed, flinging her arms around him. "I promise to keep up with my important things. Wow, if it weren't for me, you'd be a ne'er-do-well! Wait until I tell Da-Da-Doo!"

As Casey raced to her room to talk to her stuffed dragon, Bobby couldn't help but smile. He liked being a big brother.

Mr. Ellis-Chan had left Bobby's afternoon snack on the kitchen table. Today it was a chunk of cheddar cheese, some green grapes, and what looked like either a cookie or maybe mashed potatoes. Or, knowing his father, a combination of both.

"How was school?" his dad's voice said behind him.

Bobby startled. He had just buried the cookie/potato in the trash and hoped his father hadn't seen him. "Pretty good," Bobby said. "We need to bring in our costumes tomorrow for the dress rehearsal."

Worry washed over Mr. Ellis-Chan's face. "Oh," was all he said. "Um, how about we go to the fabric store? There was a little accident. Well, not an accident, but, well, we need more fabric."

"Will it be done in time?" Bobby asked. It would be embarrassing to be the only kid without a costume.

"Well, it won't be ready by tomorrow, but I promise it'll be done in time for the show."

Casey was happy to be back at Sew What. She took dozens of spools of thread from the shelves and then stacked them into towers on the floor. Bobby helped her put them back as the store lady stood over them and glared. "And make sure the colors are in the correct places," she snapped.

Once that was finished, Casey tagged along as Bobby went in search of the furry fabric. "Here it is!" Bobby called out to his father once he found it. "Ah-choo! Excuse me!" Bobby sneezed all the way to the cash register as he carried the fake fur.

The grumpy store lady frowned when she saw him and Casey, but then gasped when she recognized who was with them. "The Freezer!" she exclaimed as she tilted her head back and looked up. "Wow! Wait one moment." She dialed the phone and handed it to Mr. Ellis-Chan. "If you could just growl to my husband, he'll be thrilled. We're both big fans! Oh, and these must be your darling children. Don't they look sweet? Here, kids, have a lollipop! Have two!"

At the dress rehearsal, Holly's hair and costume were all old fashioned-y, just as one would expect of Miss Hannigan. St. James stood taller wearing his Daddy Warbucks suit, and Swoozie made the perfect Little Orphan Annie and even wore a red wig. Everyone looked like they just stepped off a Broadway stage.

Except, of course, for Bobby. Instead of a Sandy costume, he was wearing his usual — skater shorts and a Troy Eagle T-shirt.

"My father says to tell you that my costume will be done in time," Bobby mumbled to Mrs. Carlson. He kept his eyes on the ground as he spoke.

As the rehearsal progressed, Bobby got swept up in the show and forgot he wasn't dressed as a dog. His barking had never been better. He even added some yelps and a long, inspired howl that made everyone laugh. *Was this how Dad felt when he scored a touchdown?* he wondered. His sister Annie might be a good quarterback, but could she be half the mutt Bobby was? He couldn't wait for the show and imagined his father proudly telling the other parents, "See that dog? That's my boy!"

CHAPTER 15
The Big Night

The next days rushed past. The students of Room 15 practiced and practiced, and no one even complained. Not when they were asked to skip recess to rehearse, not when they had to be very quiet backstage, and not even when Mrs. Carlson announced that she wanted the boys and girls to hold hands when they took their bows.

PE had been going a lot smoother ever since Mr. Rainerhaus and Bobby had their talk. Bobby still didn't enjoy football, but at least it didn't make him want to throw up or break both wrists. However, the best thing about PE was that his teammates never got mad at him, or any other player, when they lost, which was often. The same could not be said for Jillian Zarr's team. Those girls were scary when they won, and even scarier when they lost.

The night of the show, Mr. Ellis-Chan ordered dinner from Pizza Wheels. Bobby was happy his father had done this instead of cooking, since he didn't want to risk getting a stomachache.

Bobby plucked a pepperoni off his pizza and popped it into his mouth. "Is my costume ready yet?" he asked his dad.

He had asked this every day since they bought the new material, but every day his father would just smile mysteriously and say, "Soon enough, soon enough." Now panic was starting to take over. *Isn't it already soon enough?* Bobby thought.

"Dad, you promised it would be ready for the show, and we have to leave in twenty minutes."

"The musical is tonight?" Mr. Ellis-Chan asked.

Bobby felt his stomach flip. But when his father broke into a grin, so did he. "Wait right here, son."

Soon Mr. Ellis-Chan reappeared, holding a light brownish pile of fake fur. "Here it is!" he declared.

Bobby just stared.

"Come on, try it on," his father said, holding it out to him.

Reluctantly, Bobby got into his Sandy costume. It was too tight in some places and too loose in others. He hoped it didn't look as bad as it felt.

"Well, it certainly is unique," Mrs. Ellis-Chan said. "You make a very memorable Sandy."

Casey was much less diplomatic. When she saw her brother, she started screaming, "It's a monster. A monster! A monster ate Bobby!!!"

"You don't have to wear it," Mr. Ellis-Chan said. His massive shoulders slumped. "Maybe you can wear those pajamas you have with dogs all over them."

It broke Bobby's heart to see his father looking so dejected. "No, I want to wear it," he insisted. "I'm sure it doesn't look that bad. *Ah-choo!* Let me just look at myself."

Bobby tripped over his tail twice while shuffling to the mirror. He suppressed the urge to scream. Casey was right. It looked like a monster had eaten him, and all that was left was part of his head sticking out. But Bobby had made a promise to his father and was determined to keep it — even if it was starting to make him itch.

Backstage at the Rancho Rosetta Elementary School auditorium, everyone was talking excitedly in hushed tones. When Bobby appeared, it was suddenly silent.

"I think you're in the wrong place, Bobby," Jillian Zarr finally said. "The Bigfoot musical is next door."

"Wow, you look . . . furry," Holly said, trying to cheer Bobby up.

"You look like Sandy after he's been in a fight with a mountain lion," St. James cried out. "Cool!"

Bobby tapped Chess on the shoulder. "Yikes!" Chess exclaimed when he turned around.

"Do you have it?" Bobby asked.

Chess nodded and handed over one of Wilbur's doggy biscuits. Bobby plopped the whole thing in his mouth. If he was going to be the best Sandy ever, he needed to act and think and eat like a dog.

Mrs. Carlson rushed up, and then skidded to a stop when she saw Bobby. "Oh!" was all she said. She recovered enough to add, "All right then, everyone, gather around." Bobby sneezed. "Bless you, Sandy. Now, we have a full house, so before we start, I just want to tell everyone, 'Break a leg!' You're all going to be great! Okay, places everyone!"

Annie and the orphans and others got into place. The music began, and then, just like in rehearsal, the curtains parted. Only this time there was a real audience of moms and dads, brothers and sisters, grandparents, neighbors, and all of Chess's relatives staring back at the kids onstage. There were bursts of light in the audience as camera flashes went off.

Backstage, Bobby tried not to sneeze. He wasn't going on for the first few numbers. When the sneezing got worse, the girls glared at him like he was doing it on purpose. Then Bobby started getting itchy — really itchy, but it was hard to scratch himself since he had thick paws. How did dogs manage? he wondered. Wilbur was always scratching himself, and in weird places too.

By the time it was Bobby's turn to go onstage, his eyes were watering and he could barely see. His nose was running and his sneezing was nonstop. When he tried his best to romp, things got worse. It was hard to move in his costume without ripping it, and he could barely bark.

Then Bobby felt an old, familiar sensation. Panic swept over him. He knew what it meant when he started wheezing, and once it started, there was no stopping it. Bobby struggled for air. With each attempt at a breath, the wheeze got bigger and more labored until it sounded like Darth Vader breathing in an echo chamber.

Unable to romp or bark, Bobby made the only sounds he could between wheezes . . . whimpers.

"Sandy's not supposed to cry," Daddy Warbucks hissed. Jillian Zarr was glaring at Bobby, and Holly looked worried.

But Bobby couldn't speak. It hurt as he tried to get air in and out. When he tripped over his tail and fell, the audience applauded, thinking it was part of the show. At last the song

ended, but when he didn't get up, no one, including Bobby, knew what to do. His chest was tightening and it was getting harder and harder to breathe. Finally, he managed to croak, "Help."

In a nanosecond, someone bolted from the back of the audience and shouted, "I'm coming, Bobby! Hang on!"

It was The Freezer, barreling full speed ahead. When he growled and did a flying leap onstage, Swoozie screamed and St. James fell off the edge.

In a sweeping movement, Mr. Ellis-Chan scooped his son up in his arms and then jumped off the stage over St. James. He ran right up the middle aisle of the auditorium, deposited his son in the car, handed Bobby his emergency inhaler, roared out of the parking lot, and drove straight home.

CHAPTER 16

He's Not Like Me

Invisibility. That's the superpower Bobby wished he had. It would certainly come in handy during football or school musicals. Even though he was at home now, the pain of what had just happened was so sharp that Bobby was doubled over.

Having an asthma attack was humiliating enough. But to have one onstage with an audience watching? To see your father come running up yelling, "I'm coming, Bobby! Hang on!" Then to be carried away like a baby? It was just too much.

Stupid asthma. Stupid, dumb, rotten asthma.

By now, Bobby was used to asthma attacks, but being used to something didn't necessarily mean you liked it. As he sat still on the couch with his nebulizer mask on, Bobby listened to the never-ending drone of the machine. It was a sound he hated, even though it meant that as he breathed in, the medicine was rushing into his lungs to make him better. The nebulizer reminded him of all the things he couldn't do.

It meant that he always had to be careful not to overexert himself. It meant that he couldn't have a dog, because he was allergic to fur and that could trigger an asthma attack. And, he now realized, it meant that he couldn't even *be* a dog, because he was allergic to his Sandy costume.

As wisps of mist escaped from the nebulizer, Bobby looked at his dad, who was slumped in his Laz-E-Guy recliner, gripping a football and staring off into space. Was he embarrassed that his son had stopped the musical cold by having a mega asthma attack in front of an auditorium full of people? When his father was in front of a crowd, he did amazing things like score touchdowns, not fall over and make weird noises.

Just when Mr. Ellis-Chan turned the nebulizer off and Bobby could breathe normally, the front door burst open and Mrs. Ellis-Chan and the girls rushed in.

"How are you, honey?" his mother asked. Her face was etched with worry. "We would have come home sooner, but your father took the car and Casey was scared to walk in the dark. So we got a ride home from the Harpers."

Casey nodded. "There are scary cats in the dark. Bobby, are you going to die?" She had tears in her eyes.

"No, I'm not going to die," Bobby assured her.

"Well, that was some drama!" Annie said, laughing. "It was the best part of the show. Oh man! To see Dad charging up on the stage like some superhero. Totally cool!"

Bobby felt his jaw tense. He could never face the kids at school again, not after his dad had embarrassed him like that.

"Where is your father?" Mrs. Ellis-Chan asked.

"Maybe Daddy's hiding," Casey said, peeking under the couch.

Bobby looked around for his dad. He wondered if his father had any clue how hard it was to be the son of a famous ex-football player. It was bad enough being compared to The Freezer all the time, but then to be treated like a helpless little kid was almost more than he could bear. So maybe he wasn't like Annie, Miss Big Shot Football Star, but that didn't mean that he didn't matter. "He's not like me" echoed in Bobby's head.

Bobby gathered his courage. His lungs still hurt slightly, but he wasn't going to let this stop him. He would confront his father, even if it might be painful. It was time his father knew how he felt.

After searching the house, Bobby spotted a familiar silhouette in the backyard. In the moonlight he could see his dad with his head bowed, standing near the tree where Rover was buried. Bobby took a deep breath, then marched outside.

"Dad?"

Mr. Ellis-Chan looked up. "Oh, hi, Bobby."

"Can we talk?" The cold air was bracing and Bobby was feeling brave.

"Of course, but I already know what you're going to say," his father said.

"You do?"

"Yes . . . that I'm a rotten dad."

Bobby wasn't sure he was hearing correctly. He shook his head. "What?"

"I said, 'I'm a rotten dad,'" Mr. Ellis-Chan repeated.

"No . . . I . . . you're . . . what?" Bobby's brain was on overload. This was not how he thought the conversation would begin.

"The dog costume," his father struggled to explain. "I wanted to impress you with my sewing and make you proud of me, but instead it was a disaster. Then, when it triggered your asthma attack, I realized how much I messed up."

"Well, yeah. But, no . . . I mean, that wasn't your fault. Well, it was, and it was bad, and I felt . . ." Bobby's words deserted him. He felt like everything was upside down.

"I should have known better," his dad lamented. "It's my job to take care of you, not to put you in danger. What kind of father does that?"

"Dad," Bobby tried again. He had to remind himself of what he had wanted to say. "I know you were trying to do a good thing when you made my costume, but when I had my asthma attack, you didn't think about how it would make me feel if you . . ."

Bobby stopped when he saw his father's face. He was used to his dad looking big and brave and having everything under control — well, except for cooking and cleaning and stuff like that. But here was a dad who looked like he needed some help. Bobby didn't know if he should confront his father or console him.

Mr. Ellis-Chan's eyes met Bobby's. For a moment, no one spoke. Then Bobby took a deep breath and said, "Dad, you're doing great."

"I am?" Mr. Ellis-Chan said, sounding surprised and pleased. "Well, it's hard. There are no lessons on how to be a dad, unlike football, where they train you. You know, Bobby, I spent practically my whole life focused on becoming a pro football player, and I loved it. But it was scary too. I was traded a couple of times before I landed with the Earthquakes. . . ." Bobby had sort of known about that, but had never given it any thought. His father continued. "I thought I had finally found a home, a team, where I would have been happy to stay forever. Then one day, BAM. I got my knee blown out and it was over. I felt lost."

"You felt lost?" Bobby asked. He thought he was the only one in the Ellis-Chan family who ever felt that way.

"Sure," his father said. "I was at the top of my game, then the game was over before I was ready. After that, I had that job, remember?"

Bobby nodded. The Freezer had been the spokesman for a chain of sporting good stores, but hadn't been very good at it and was let go.

"Well, when your mom and I decided that I would become a stay-at-home dad, I thought, 'Now here's something I can do really well!' I knew I couldn't get fired from that job and I was determined to be the best stay-at-home dad ever. That's why when I cook, I don't just make plain pancakes, I make apple banana crunch pancakes! Instead of meat loaf, I make fish and hamburger loaf! And instead of spaghetti and meatballs, I make meatballs filled with spaghetti. . . ."

"Um, Dad?" Bobby interrupted. "You know what? Plain is fine. We don't mind."

"Really?" His father looked surprised. "Because, honestly, that would be easier." He gave it some thought. "Hey, if I spend less time in the kitchen, I could spend more time with you. We could go outside and . . ."

Before his father could say, "play football," Bobby cut in. Now was the time to tell him. "Dad, um, maybe you haven't noticed, but I'm not the greatest at football. I mean, I'm not like you, or even Annie. But I know you already know that. I heard you say it."

"Say what?" his father asked, looking confused.

Bobby's throat was dry, but his eyes began to water. "That day that I took a dive to avoid getting hit by Annie's pass," he said, gathering his courage. "Later, as I was doing an ollie and you were doing push-ups, I heard you talking about me to Annie. You told her, 'He's not like me.' And then she said, 'That's for sure.'"

There. Bobby had said it. It felt good to have gotten it out, but rotten at the same time. He knew his father would never fire him, but when Mr. Ellis-Chan didn't say anything, Bobby worried that his dad might want to trade him to another team.

"Son," Mr. Ellis-Chan said gently. Bobby looked up. His father didn't look angry or disgusted; instead, he looked concerned. "What I was telling Annie was that I was proud of you. I could never skateboard as well as you. All those tricks you can do — they amaze me. I'm so big and clumsy on a skateboard. . . . I'm not like you."

Bobby was speechless. *That* was what his father meant?

"But — but," Bobby stammered, "I thought you were ashamed that I'm not big and strong like you, and that I'm horrible at football."

Mr. Ellis-Chan mussed up Bobby's hair. "You've still got a lot of growing ahead of you. I was small when I was your age."

"You were?" Bobby asked.

His father nodded. "Bobby," he said, "I don't expect you to be a football player, and I wouldn't want you to be one."

"You wouldn't?"

"Not unless you really wanted to."

"Yes, but you're so proud that Annie's the quarterback."

"I am proud," Mr. Ellis-Chan said, "because that's what she wants to do. Annie has worked really hard to achieve her goal. But I'm proud of you too."

"Why?" Bobby asked. "We're so different."

"Well, how much time do you have?" his dad quipped. "You're a great big brother to Casey. I don't know anyone who could be as patient with her as you are." Bobby nodded. That was true. "And you have a lot of friends." Bobby nodded again. "Plus, your skateboarding is amazing. I am in awe of what you can do. And, I admit, I am slightly jealous of Troy Eagle."

"You are?" This surprised Bobby.

"Sure," his dad admitted. "I mean, you have that huge Troy Eagle poster in your room, and you talk about him all the time. I know you really look up to him and that he's your hero." He paused. "Listen, Bobby, I love you so much. It means a lot to me to hear that you don't think I'm a failure as a dad. 'Cause you know what? I'd do anything for you. I'd fight a hundred tigers . . . I'd climb a thousand mountains. . . . I'd even eat a million bugs for you."

"You would?" Bobby asked.

"Yup."

Bobby nodded. "I'd do the same for you, Dad," he said, then added, "but I might use ketchup on the bugs."

Mr. Ellis-Chan let out a huge roar of laughter as he wrapped Bobby in a bear hug. "Well, son, you see, we're not that different after all."

CHAPTER 17
Stupid Rotten Asthma

The next morning, Bobby was lying on the couch. It was supremely uncomfortable since he was also wearing his backpack, but he didn't feel like moving. Besides, Casey was listening to his elbow with her stethoscope.

"Bobby," his mother said. She was wearing her cerulean-colored suit, which meant she had a big meeting. "Honey, I know you don't want to go to school, but you have to."

"I can't," he said, sitting up. That made his back feel better. "Everyone's going to make fun of me."

"No one's going to make fun of you for having an asthma attack," his mother assured him.

"That's not true," Annie said as she strolled through the living room, clutching her books. "Someone's sure to make fun of him. I know it was serious. I've seen enough of Bobby's asthma attacks. But if you've never seen one before, it looks and sounds kinda weird." Bobby flopped back down on the couch. "But if anyone makes fun of you," Annie added, "send them to me and I'll make sure they never tease you again."

"I can fight my own battles," Bobby grumbled.

"Sheesh!" Annie cried. "I was just trying to be nice. Then let them make fun of you. See if I care!"

Now Bobby felt doubly bad. He didn't like it when Annie was mad at him.

"Come on," Mrs. Ellis-Chan said, helping him up. "Fourth grade awaits."

"He can't go," Casey shouted as she gave him a pretend shot. "I'm Dr. Princess Becky and I say that Bobby has the chicken pops!"

"I'll be okay," he told Casey. Mr. Ellis-Chan came in from the kitchen and handed him his lunch. "Are we still on for today?" Bobby asked his dad.

When he got a thumbs-up, he felt a little bit better.

By the time he got to Holly's house, he was ten minutes late. Holly had her arms crossed and was tapping her foot.

"Sorry," Bobby apologized as Holly looked at her watch.

"Oh, that's all right," she said. Holly had a hard time staying mad at Bobby. "We'll just have to walk fast."

Bobby ran to catch up to her. "What happened after I left the show?" he asked, even though he wasn't sure that he really wanted to know.

"Well," Holly started, "at first no one knew what to do. Then Mrs. Carlson apologized, saying there was a medical emergency. Then the show went on and it was great!" Her eyes were bright.

"But what about Sandy? Who took my part?" Bobby asked. He wondered if maybe Chess stepped in for him. Chess was pretty good at being a dog, although his romping could use some work.

"We just did the musical without Sandy," Holly explained. "Don't worry, it was fine. No one noticed you weren't there."

Bobby felt like he had been slugged. The show went on without him and nobody noticed?

"Oh, Bobby," Holly continued, "it was so fun! We got a standing ovation."

Bobby pretended to smile, even though he felt lousy. *Stupid rotten asthma,* he thought. He had always wanted a standing ovation. Sometimes, when he was alone in his room, he practiced taking bows in front of an imaginary audience.

Holly and Bobby slipped into Room 15 just as everyone was settling down. Several of the girls snickered when they saw him. Chess was organizing his pencils. He did this every morning. "You okay?" he asked without looking up.

"I guess," Bobby answered.

"I fell off the stage," St. James boasted. "Your dad is so cool. Did you see how he leapt over those people? He's like Super Football Dude. You should have seen your face when he was carrying you like a football. You looked so weird."

"Yeah," another boy added, "I would have been so embarrassed if my dad did that. I'm surprised you even showed up to school today."

"And those freaky sounds you were making, it sounded like a wounded animal," someone else added. "Can you teach me how to do it?"

Bobby felt himself shrinking. Maybe he'd turn invisible after all.

"You could have waited until you were backstage," Jillian Zarr sniffed. "But noooo, you had to cause a big scene and disrupt the entire show. That's so like you, Bobby Ellis-Chan. You're just an attention hog and so is your father. My mother even said so."

Bobby winced. "Jillian Zarr, for your information, I don't have asthma attacks on purpose," he protested. "And as for my dad, he was just trying to help me!"

Just then, Mrs. Carlson approached his desk. "I'm so happy to see you're all right. I was worried about you. Bobby, why don't you explain to the class what asthma is?"

Bobby gulped. It was bad enough they saw an asthma attack in action — but now he was expected to talk about it?

Mrs. Carlson smiled encouragingly.

He took in a deep breath and looked directly at Jillian Zarr. "First of all, I can't help it when I get asthma attacks. Asthma's this thing, a disease —" He cringed when he heard someone say, "Eeeew, Bobby has a disease."

Mrs. Carlson nodded to him to keep going.

"It means that if I have a bad allergic reaction to something, or a cough, it can trigger my asthma," he explained. "When that happens, I start wheezing —"

"Like this!" St. James said, demonstrating wheezing. Soon all the boys were making wheezing noises.

"Thank you, boys," Mrs. Carlson said. "But that's enough. Bobby, please continue."

"Well, when I wheeze, my chest really hurts, like someone's pressing on it and I can't get enough air. Then I have to go on my nebulizer —"

"That's a machine," Chess jumped in. "I've seen it many times. It's like some space alien contraption that delivers medicine."

Bobby nodded. He'd often thought of his nebulizer that way.

Mrs. Carlson stood behind Bobby. "Class, I think we can all agree that Bobby is very brave to have to put up with all of this. Lots of people have medical conditions that they've learned to live with. If we can be more understanding of others, everyone benefits."

Just then Swoozie raised her hand. "Mrs. Carlson, my brother has diabetes."

Soon everyone was discussing their medical ailments and showing off their bruises and scars. One girl had her tonsils out, and another got hives whenever she ate strawberries. St. James showed the class his scrapes from when he fell off the stage, and Jackson said he had a lactose intolerance and couldn't drink milk, but he was almost certain that ice cream was okay. Bobby was glad that the spotlight was off of him.

"All right then," Mrs. Carlson said. "I want to thank everyone for sharing. I hope that now that we know more about one another, we'll be less likely to make fun of someone if something happens that they have no control over."

Bobby glanced at Jillian Zarr, but she was busy looking at her fingernails.

"Now then," Mrs. Carlson announced. "We got our class pictures back! I'm going to pass them out so you can see them, but then I want them kept in your desk until it's time to go home."

The front row began laughing and by the time the students in back of the room got their pictures, everyone had turned around to look at Bobby. Slowly, he turned the photo over, and then understood why.

Bobby turned to St. James. "You said we ALL were going to make faces."

"I said that?" St. James asked innocently.

Chess looked apologetic. "I was going to," he said, "but I chickened out. After all, my mom's going to see this."

Bobby groaned and stuffed the photo in his desk. Great. Was this how he was going to be remembered in fourth grade?

At recess, Jillian Zarr's wolf pack circled Bobby. "First you make all the boys wear their shirts backward and inside out, then you sabotage the musical, and now this! You ruined the class photo!" Jillian cried.

All the girls mimicked the face that Bobby had made in the class photo.

"Bobby Ellis-Chan, you are a disgrace!" Jillian Zarr announced. "Can't you do anything right?"

Bobby glanced around for reinforcements, but the rest of the guys were at the far end of the playground playing Arctic ice robots. Jillian Zarr's stare was making him start to wither. Then his eyes met Holly's. She didn't look angry, like the rest of the girls. She looked straight at him and gave him a nod so small that he was sure no one else had seen it. But it was all he needed.

Standing up straight, Bobby said to Jillian Zarr, "I am not a disgrace. I am Bobby Ellis-Chan, and if you don't like that, then you can . . . you can . . . you can just go back to Mars!" And with that, Bobby turned on his heels and went to join the boys, as Jillian Zarr stood speechless.

CHAPTER 18
In Sync

For the first time in his life, Bobby was looking forward to PE.

"What's going on?" Holly asked as the teams lined up and Mr. Rainerhaus took roll.

"Nothing," Bobby said, trying to hide a grin.

"Bobby Ellis-Chan, I know you," she said, shaking her head. "You're up to something."

Just then, a loud, deep voice yelled, "Where's Mr. Rainerhaus?"

Everyone froze as a large figure in full football gear stampeded toward Mr. Rainerhaus. It stopped short of knocking him over, and growled with one arm out in the trademarked Freezer stance.

Elated, Mr. Rainerhaus stuck his arm out and growled back. "Everyone!" he cried. "It's Roy Ellis-Chan, The Freezer!"

The kids clapped and crowded around Bobby's dad. He normally looked big, but when he was in his LA Earthquakes uniform with all the pads, he was even more impressive.

As The Freezer gave the class tips on throwing and catching the football, Bobby watched carefully. Everyone was listening to his father and laughing and nodding. And Mr. Ellis-Chan looked happy, unlike when he burned dinner, or ruined the laundry, or sewed a dog costume.

"If it's okay with your teacher, I brought something for all of you," The Freezer was saying. Mr. Rainerhaus nodded, then beamed when Bobby's father opened a big cloth sack. Inside were special edition Freezer foam LA Earthquakes footballs. There were enough for everyone. Bobby knew the Ellis-Chan garage was full of boxes of Freezer footballs, Freezer posters, Freezer jerseys, and tons of other Freezer stuff from when his dad played pro ball.

"Bobby, will you be in charge of handing all this out?" his father asked.

"Sure thing, Dad!" Bobby said.

"My son said you were playing football, and suggested I come by," The Freezer explained to Mr. Rainerhaus as the

kids tested their new footballs. "When Bobby asks me to do something, I do it!"

"Wow," St. James told Bobby as he caught Jillian Zarr's football and then threw it over the fence. "You sure are lucky."

Bobby nodded. He did feel lucky.

That afternoon, Bobby raced to his bedroom. Next to the poster of Troy Eagle doing his record-setting ollie, Bobby put up another poster: This one was of The Freezer flying through the air, catching a football.

"Halloween's this weekend," he told Koloff and Beatrice as he stood back and admired the posters. "I'm still not sure what my costume's going to be. I know for sure it won't be Sandy the dog." Bobby took the little soccer ball out of the cigar box. "Are you ready to practice?"

When neither fish responded, he said, "What? Are you trying to tell me you don't want to do tricks? Sure you do! You should have seen all the amazing things Rover could do with this soccer ball." Beatrice turned away and explored the castle, while Koloff just stared at Bobby. "Come on you two, you can be exactly like Rover —"

Suddenly the smile fell off of Bobby's face. In shock, he sat down on his bed and stared straight ahead. Then he got up and went over to the aquarium. "Oh man, I owe you two an apology," he told the goldfish. "I was trying to get you to do tricks like Rover, but that was what *I* wanted, not what *you* wanted. I am so sorry. Here, look!" Bobby took the ball and the hoops out of the fish tank. "See, you don't have to do tricks. Not if you don't want to. Really, I promise. You two are terrific just the way you are!"

Upon hearing this, Beatrice swam up to the top of the fish tank, and Koloff joined her. Then together they swam to the bottom and, side by side, circled the tank twice before returning to the surface.

"What was that?" Bobby asked.

Again, the fish swam side by side, this time doing flips and spins along the way.

Bobby couldn't believe what he was seeing.

Koloff and Beatrice were dancing.

The outside of the Ellis-Chan house was decorated with not-too-scary skeletons and big pumpkins carved to look like

Annie, Bobby, and Casey. Fake friendly bats hung from the rafters of the front porch and sparkly cobwebs adorned the windows. Mr. Ellis-Chan secured a giant spider made from plastic garbage bags to the roof as Annie raked the leaves off the lawn and then put up fake tombstones.

Inside, Mrs. Ellis-Chan, Bobby, and Casey were seated around the kitchen table. In the middle were piles of individually wrapped gumballs, fun-sized chocolate bars, and sparkly Go Girly Girl stickers.

"You still haven't told me what your costume is," Bobby said to Casey. He popped an orange gumball into his mouth, then blew a bubble. Bobby was good at blowing bubbles. Sometimes they got so big that the gum got stuck in his hair.

"Guess! Bobby, guess who I'm going to be for Halloween!" Casey said as she slapped a sticker on her forehead and then one on his.

Bobby pretended to think about it. "Princess Becky?" It was a pretty safe bet, since that's who Casey dressed as every day.

"Nope." She giggled. "You'll see."

"What about you, Bobby?" Mrs. Ellis-Chan asked as she dropped a gumball, a chocolate, and some stickers into a bag and then tied a ribbon around it. "Since you can't wear your Sandy costume, we can run to the store, or maybe cobble together something from home. How about your space alien costume from last year? Does that still fit?"

"One of the heads fell off," he informed his mother. Bobby snuck his fifth gumball. It was getting hard to talk. "But don't worry about it. I have something else in mind."

After the bags were filled, Bobby went into the yard to admire the tombstones. Casey was talking to Wormy Worm Worm as Gnomey Gnome Gnome stood quietly off to the side.

Bobby picked up the gnome. "Casey," he said. "This doesn't belong to you."

"I know," she said. "I gave it to my worm."

He shook his head. "You took it from someone's yard, and now you have to give it back."

Casey's eyes filled with tears. "But Bobby, Mommy said she wanted something for her garden. Plus, that's Wormy Worm Worm's best friend."

"I thought *you* were Wormy Worm Worm's best friend," he said.

Casey smiled. "I am!" she said gleefully. "I guess I forgot."

"Come on, Casey," he said. "I'll help you make something for Mom's garden later. In the meantime, let's ask Holly to take us back to where this lawn gnome lives. He's been on vacation long enough."

"Swoozie lives there," Holly said, pointing to a tidy two-story brick house with a lady lawn gnome and three smaller gnomes standing next to her in the garden.

Bobby could see a brown patch on the grass where another lawn gnome had once stood. "Put him back, Casey," he instructed.

Reluctantly, his sister shuffled over to the brown patch, holding Gnomey Gnome Gnome. She kissed his head, then returned him to his family.

As they walked back, Casey's lower lip began to quiver. "I miss Gnomey Gnome Gnome."

"Well, I'm sure he's happy to be home," Holly told her. "You can visit him anytime."

Casey brightened at the thought. "Hey, Holly Holly Holly, did you know that Beatrice and Koloff can dance?"

Holly smiled. "That's nice, Casey," she said.

"It's true!" Bobby told her. "Come on, I'll show you. Let's race to my house!"

Holly peered into the aquarium. Then she rubbed her eyes and looked again. "Bobby! It really does look like they're doing synchronized swimming."

Casey pressed her nose against the glass. "What's stinkronized swimming? Does it hurt? Does it stink? Holly, did you know that fish poop and pee in the water?"

"Casey, stop that," Bobby said, wiping her nose print off the glass. "*Synchronized* swimming is like dancing in the water together. See how Koloff and Beatrice are swimming side by side?"

"Can they twirl?" Casey asked. "I can." She twirled around the room to prove it.

"It's amazing," Holly gushed as Casey spun past her. "How did you get Beatrice and Koloff to swim together?"

"I didn't do anything," Bobby said. "I kept trying to get them to do Rover's tricks, but they weren't interested. This was all their idea."

Casey twirled past again, then fell over. When no one said anything, she leapt up and fell over again, then got up and left in a huff.

"I'm going to wear my Miss Hannigan costume tonight," Holly told Bobby. "What are you going to be for Halloween?"

"All the guys are going as superheroes this year. I'm going as one too," Bobby said.

CHAPTER 19
Superheroes

It was starting to get dark outside as the Ellis-Chans scarfed down their dinner of bologna-and-cheese sandwiches and carrot sticks. Annie was wearing a Glinda the Good Witch costume, and Mrs. Ellis-Chan looked like a giant apple.

"You guys better get dressed for Halloween," Annie said. She drained a glass of milk and then belched. "There's not that much time."

Mr. Ellis-Chan, Casey, and Bobby all stopped chewing, then abandoned their meals and raced up the stairs.

After changing into his costume, Bobby flexed his muscles, admired himself in the mirror, and then took a bow as the imaginary audience cheered. "Well, what do you two think?" he asked Koloff and Beatrice. They swam side by side, then spun around.

When Bobby went back downstairs, he was shocked to see what was waiting for him in the living room. His father stared back at Bobby and appeared to be in shock too.

Mr. Ellis-Chan was wearing a Troy Eagle skateboard shirt, skater shorts, a brain bucket, and kneepads!

"I don't have a skateboard," Bobby's dad said, "so I patched this one up." He held up the broken Troy Eagle Super 74. It looked like there were miles of gray duct tape wrapped around it. "I hope you approve of my Bobby Ellis-Chan costume."

A huge grin crossed Bobby's face. "I approve," he said, motioning to his own costume. "Do you?"

Mr. Ellis-Chan's grin mirrored his son's. "I approve a hundred and fifty percent," he said, holding out his hand so Bobby could give him a high five.

Bobby was wearing a LA Earthquakes jersey with number 17 on it — his dad's number. Plus he had borrowed Annie's helmet and pads and was holding a Freezer football.

Annie strolled into the room carrying a giant cauldron filled with bags of treats. "Well, you two look weird," she said. Bobby thought she looked really pretty in her Glinda costume, but didn't say anything for fear she'd slug him.

"I think we all look great!" Mrs. Ellis-Chan said as she joined them. "But what about Casey — where is she?"

"I'm almost ready!" they heard Casey shout from her room.

The family gathered at the bottom of the stairs to wait for Casey's grand entrance. "Get ready," she called out. "Get set. . . . Look at me!!!"

"Where's your costume?" Bobby asked when his little sister joined the rest of the family.

"This is it," Casey replied, striking a pose like a fashion model.

"What are you supposed to be?"

"A regular girl," Casey answered matter-of-factly. "It's a costume, Bobby. It's *pretend*!" Instead of her usual Princess Becky gown, sparkly shoes, crown, and Wandee II, she was wearing jeans, a sweater, and tennis shoes. "No one will ever know it's me!" Casey whispered.

"Okay," Bobby whispered back. "It'll be our secret."

The sidewalks of Rancho Rosetta were crammed full of kids and their parents. All the houses were lit up inside, making them look like giant jack-o'-lanterns. Laughter and squeals of joy filled the air. In the distance, Bobby could see Chess and the guys making their way toward him.

As the Ellis-Chans joined the rest of the trick-or-treaters, Casey perked up when she saw a familiar face. "Holly Holly Holly," she shouted, running to catch up to her. "Holly, try to guess who I am! I'll give you a hint . . . it's me, Casey!"

Bobby and his father exchanged smiles. All around them were astronauts and aliens, princesses and pirates. But as far as they could see there were only two real superheroes — a football player and a skateboarder.

CHECK OUT ALL OF LISA YEE'S SO TOTALLY FUNNY BOOKS!

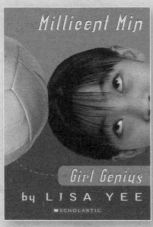

"Hilarious."
—*Miami Herald*

"Funny and sweet."
—*The New York Times*

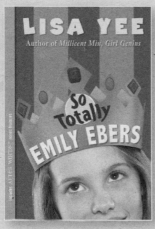

"[A] great read."
—teensreadtoo.com

"Funny...touching."
—*Booklist*